BITCH
we can Share
PART I

Chenette Whitfield

authorHOUSE

AuthorHouse™
1663 Liberty Drive
Bloomington, IN 47403
www.authorhouse.com
Phone: 1-800-839-8640

First published by AuthorHouse 3/12/2010

ISBN: 978-1-4490-8749-4 (e)
ISBN: 978-1-4490-8748-7 (sc)

Printed in the United States of America
Bloomington, Indiana

This book is printed on acid-free paper.

Contents

Chapter One

"Two hundred in five. That's what I'm talking about. Ya'll can't fuck wit me in this bowling shit!" yelled Sequoia jumping up out her seat in front of the wall mounted High Definition television. " Bitch I can still catch you. We only in the fifth", said Zikhya. The girls were in Zikhya's living room playing Wii Sports on the Wii Nintendo system. They had a ball the night before at RAMS head when they went to see Lil Wayne live. The bitches were dressed bad, hands down. Sequoia Birmingham-Wallace stood five foot even with wide hips and thick toned thighs. She had a complex bout being so small up top, but knew she made up for that with her humungous ass. She wore a white Elizabeth Taylor ruffle layered baby doll blouse that went well with her Twix candy bar complexion. She wore Christian Dior skinny jeans and four inch Manolo high heels. She topped her outfit off with her white Gucci shades and wore her long hair in a neat ponytail. The men at the concert definitely knew how to strike her twenty seven year old ego, but she was very well married. Zikhya Palms, twenty nine stood four foot four and was as light as a stick of butter. She was extremely top and bottom heavy with a glow to her smooth yellow skin. After her brother Zonado was brutally murdered, she put all of her pain into working out at Curves and it definitely paid off. Zikhya was a huge fan of Lil Wayne so she was the most excited. She even tore her Prada G-string off and threw it on stage. Surprisingly, Lil Wayne picked them up, sniffed them, and put them in his back pocket where his red bandana hung. Suddenly, every female followed suit, only they had angry husbands and boyfriends to answer to. Zikhya didn't have that problem and planned to keep it that way. She wore a sheer one piece cat suit with pastels covering her nipples matched with a black pair of Girbaud wedge heels. Her hair fell beautifully in soft waves. Raleigh McDowell, thirty years of age standing five foot three, was the darker of the four girls. There was no denying that Raleigh was the prettiest dark skinned female that most people ever saw, her appearance always remained flawless. She wore a pink and grey sweater dress accentuated with a pair of grey suede Burberry high heels. Last but not least, Menijah

Jones, twenty eight stood five foot three with a Halle Berry complexion. She wore a white Fendi mini skirt, a black sleeveless Marc Jacob turtle neck sweater, and zebra print four inch Apple Bottom high heels. She wore her hair bone straight down to her waist, courtesy of her Hibachi Indian heritage.

The girls always did everything together so when Sequoia became married, the friends couldn't deny that things had changed drastically. Although Raleigh and Zikhya were secretly jealous because Sequoia was married, they accepted Morton Wallace also known as Mo-T on the streets of Baltimore, as long as he treated her good. Mo-T tried explaining to his wife that he feels that when a couple is married that they should affiliate with people of that same nature, but Sequoia wasn't trying to hear it. Unbeknownst to her, she would soon regret her decision. The girls had Mo-T drop them off and caught a cab back to Zikhya's house. Sequoia was so drunk; she wouldn't even have been able to tell anyone the year she was born. Raleigh and Menijah resided with Zikhya as well. They were tired of men running game on them so of course Zikhya opened up her home to them. Their stay was rent and utility free. All that Zikhya asked of them was for them to clean up behind their self because she wasn't cleaning after grown ass women. Zikhya lived in a four bedroom home in the Pikesville community in Baltimore. The house featured an in ground pool, a day room, a finished basement with a wet-bar, a pool table, and a stripper pole. The kitchen's counter tops were designed as marble, featuring a breakfast bar, an island in the middle of the kitchen, a whirlpool refrigerator with a built in television. The living room was all mirrors including on the ceiling, decorated with a nineteenth century Persian rug. The white and gold Russian signature furniture set pretty in its position. It was something off of MTV cribs. On the ride to Zikhya's palce, the girls gave the cab driver the blues. " Mothafucka you better take us where we going too "slurred Raleigh. She was the hot head of the crew. Zikhya, Menijah, and Sequoia laughed, as they were all drunk as well. " Naw, Raleigh, I don't think he ant these problems. I think he knows better", said Menijah. " Man, that tight ass prince leather with that played out Islam turban he got on his head. Plus he got that gay ass Michael Jackson earring in his ear!" laughed Zikhya. The pecan complexioned cab driver with a low wavy haircut, neatly shaped up, perfect set of white teeth looked at Zikhya through his rearview mirror as the girls doubled over in laughter. Honestly to him, Zikhya was the most attractive one of the four. He thought of the about the chances of seeing her again, which were slim to none.

On second thought, he knew that the destination he was now arriving to was some sort of connection to the beauty. He knew trying to rap to her while she was drunk and with her home girls wouldn't be the right approach. He watched the stumble up the driveway laughing. Zikhya turned around barely able to stand up, put her middle finger up at the cab driver and tripped on her own feet into the house.

"Man, I'm going to miss ya'll when I fly to Las Vegas to do those photo shoots for VIBE", said Sequoia pretending to pout like a child. It wasn't like her and Mo-T was hurting for money, Mo-T was dedicated to the hustle of the streets. Sequoia didn't approve, but she loved her husband and stood behind him no matter what. To Mo-T money was money and he had lots of it. That's why he didn't understand why Sequoia wanted to experience working. Sequoia didn't know what it was like to pay a bill, let alone work. All she knew was cash, shopping and just plain living good. However, Mo-T didn't realize that Sequoia accepted the invitation for experience. Everything was given to her and she felt it was time to earn something on her own. Experience and knowledge isn't materialistic, it can't be taken away from you once you grasp it. She considered it as an opportunity and she took advantage of it. After finally getting Mo-T to finally agree to let her go, she promised to call him every chance she got. He was happy she wasn't taking Menijah, Raleigh, and Zikhya with her. Of course Mo-T did her share of crut to her and like every woman who's blinded by love, she stuck by him for nine long years. It was all in the name of love. Sequoia knew she was drop dead gorgeous, top of the line bitch, but love don't care what you look like. "Bitch I don't see why you can't take us with you" said Menijah dropping down on the floor and holding onto her leg. " Bitch get up "laughed Sequoia. " I mean forreal, shit, who wouldn't want this body on the front of their magazine?" said Zikhya posing in the diamond cut floor length mirror in living room. " Bitch well I didn't even know they saw me until VIBE mailed those free flight tickets to the house "said Sequoia. " That's wassup" said Zikhya and Raleigh. " Well let me go home and deal with Morton's bullshit" said Sequoia. " That's wassup", said Zikhya and Raleigh. " Fucking wit ya'll at that Lil Wayne concert last night, I got go hear Morton's bullshit" said Sequoia looking in the mirror checking her hair, make-up and turning to the side to see how her ass looked in her Ed Hardy jeans. She brushed her peach crissed crossed back designed Baby Phat blouse, checked her peach and white jordans on her feet and grabbed her keys. " Okay ya'll I think my cab is out there. I get up wit ya'll later "said Sequoia opening the door to exit.

"Morton I was fucking drunk! I couldn't even call Jesus Christ is I wanted to because I was so drunk!" yelled Sequoia. In the middle of their arguing, she noticed that Morton had packed her Luivuitton luggage for her trip. He could be so sweet when he wanted to. "Bitch you probably had some nigga feeling up and feeding you some bullshit that you fell for! You think I trust them tramp ass skeezers you call yourself having for friends!" yelled Mo-T getting up in Sequoia's face. She saw veins and sweating popping out of his face and knew not to fuck with him. She was crazy, but she wasn't stupid. " Oh so that's what the fuck you think you did to me when we met? That's what the fuck you think made me give you nine years of my life Morton" asked Sequoia with a tremble in her voice. As tears slid down her face, Mo-T walked away because he hated it when she cried. She grabbed her luggage, headed out of the garage, got in her Dodge Caliber and drove to BWI airport. Mo-T had pride but it was no doubt that it fucked his head up to see his wife hurting. He had hurt her enough with his bullshit for nine years, but Mo-T was a man first before he was anything and her had somehow made Sequoia believe his bullshit ass logic. He selfishly married her to assure himself that her had her for life, not willing to give her the same security. In Mo-T's head, for every man there were at least twenty women if not more. He believed that it was a man's world. Sequoia never threatened to cheat or leave and he gave her mad respect for that. He couldn't say the same for a lot of the immature bitches he was fucking with. Mo-T knew what he had in Sequoia and she wasn't stupid like her so called friends said she was because she put up with his bullshit. She was simply in love with her husband and that was something that those bottom of the barrel freaks knew nothing about. Mo-T couldn't lie, the bitches were bad, far from average. Sequoia was down to ride and that's why he made it his business to tie her down for life. She would just have to hurt until he was done with the life, after all, love is pain. He decided to wait until she calmed down to call her and apology for upsetting her. Her turned out all the lights in their large bedroom and laid back in their king size sleigh bed watching ESPN on the seventy five inch wall mounted plasma High Definition flat screen television.

"Mo-T always popping' shit", said Raleigh . " I know, like he forgetting we the bitches that always had your back when shit got thick. He know what it is "said Zikhya. "Sequoia tell Mo-T he acting like a real pussy", said Menijah. Sequoia called her girls on her way to the airport to tell them about the argument with Mo-T. " I know ya'll and he really hurt my feelings with that bullshit. Then later he'll be calling me apologizing "said Sequoia still upset. " He need a bitch like me "Zikhya whispered in Raleigh's ear so Sequoia couldn't here. Menijah was sitting on the floor while they were on the bed, so she couldn't here what they said. She just brushed it off as nothing and continued cleaning underneath her fingernails. Zikhya knew that if Menijah knew anything she would tell Sequoia. She knew that whatever Zikhya said . Raleigh giggled and nodded her head in agreement. " You've been accepting his apologies for nine years so why wouldn't he?" Menijah yelled into the speakerphone. " I know. Well I'm at the airport so I'll holler at ya'll when I touchdown in Vegas "said Sequoia. " We love you!" they all yelled through the speakerphone. Sequoia laughed. " Okay, bye" . For some reason she got a funny feeling in her stomach, but couldn't quite figure out why. She just felt that something wasn't quite right. She decided to ignore it. Besides his infedelities, she had the most wonderful husband in the world and had three best friends that were like sisters. What could possibly be wrong?

Chapter Two

"Oh yeah I like these Banana Republic jeans. They fit me just right", said Menijah looking in the mirror at her butt. " I'm rollin wit these Dereon jeans. They the only brand that fit me straight", said Raleigh holding her jeans in her hands as she stood outside of Menijah's dressing room stall. The girls were bored without Sequoia and decided to go out. They were shopping at the Hagerstown Maryland clothing outlet. " I'm rocking this white Marc Jacob one piece jumper with my burgundy Christian Dior wide hip belt and my burgundy snake skin stilettos. I'll be at the register" said Zikhya. Besides partying and having fun, Zikhya had a mission she wanted to accomplish that night after the club. She didn't want to waste anytime seducing Mo-T because she figured the sooner the better. Although her secret was safe with Raleigh, she knew she had to be careful not to let Menijah get wind of her plan. Zikhya knew Raleigh had a thing for Mo-T as well but, she wouldn't dare make a move without Zikhya. Menijah on the other hand was a flat out snitch, and they had to learn that the hard way. Back in the day, they used to boost clothes and one day they got caught. After the detectives put pressure on Menijah asking who was the mastermind behind the whole idea, she broke down and ratted Zikhya out. Since then, they all knew where they stood with Menijah. The problem was that Zikhya wasn't trying to share Mo-T with Raleigh. She wanted him all for herself before Sequoia returned from Las Vegas. Zikhya remembered when Mo-T and Sequoia first met. It was Menijah's birthday and they took her on a cruise to the Caribbean Island. They were all on the boat getting twisted that night when they spotted Mo-T and his boys. " Damn, look at him "said Zikhya referring to Mo-T. Menijah, Raleigh, and Sequoia mouths hung open as they spotted the Mekhi Pheifer look alike. He had a body like Usher and swag like The Game. " Come on, let's walk past him and his crew "said Raleigh. As soon as the girls attempted to switch past, Mo-T and his crew stepped directly in front of them blocking their paths. It was way more of his homeboys than it was them, so everybody just grabbed who they wanted. Unfortunately, Mo-T didn't grab Zikhya. She was disappointed, but refused to show it. She continued to have a nice time and work with the guy she had. He was a sexy Arabic ethnic guy looking to be in his forties. He looked like something that just dropped out of heaven and had the body of a goddess. His long silky hair fell down his back in a ponytail and his perfect set of white teeth were shining as he smiled. Zikhya had to wonder what this guy was doing hanging out with someone like Mo-T. then again with Mo-T, you never knew. He knew all kinds of people. For the cruise, the girls all decided to wear Ball Gowns the first night of their arrival as Menijah's birthday theme. Raleigh wore double criss cross spaghetti strap lavender gown that hung down to her feet. She had a small opening at the chest of the dress reveling a little extra cleavage and complimented her dress with four inch Luivoitton glass high hell slippers. To top it off, she placed a Lilac flower in her hair which was pulled back into a neat bun. Zikhya's gown stopped right above her knees showing off her smooth golden legs. Her gown was powder blue with gold trimming. The gown was strapless and had a built in bustier with ruffles at the bottom. It fit Zikhya perfectly as if it was made especially for her. She wore gold six inch open toe Jimmy Choo high heels and let her hair fall down her back in pretty Spanish crimps. Menijah's gown was rose pink with a train attached at the bottom. Looking at the front of her dress you saw nothing outstanding about it, but the back of the dress was a different story. Menijah had a large opening showing the very top of her back all the way down to the top of her ass cheeks. She wore her hair bone straight hanging down to her waist. Last but not least, Sequoia's gown was the most stunning. Her peach gown was floor length with a V split starting at her mid thighs that caused the dress to hang on each side of her. The peach gown had silver trimming, one wide strap on the shoulder, and at the stomach the dress material was cut out into a diamond encrusted S that stood for her name. She wore silver elbow length gloves and silver Chanel stilettos. It seemed as if Sequoia and Mo-T clicked right away so Zikhya left well enough alone. She never could have guessed that nine years later Sequoia would still be on Mo-T's nuts. Behind Sequoia's back, Zikhya had tried to get wit Mo-T with her sidekick Raleigh in tote, but it was to no avail. She had to give it to Sequoia, she was smart enough to not talk about her sex life with Mo-T no matter hard the girls pushed. To Zikhya, that only meant one thing: he was laying the pipe! She would soon find out for herself and with Sequoia away this would be the perfect opportunity.

"Bitch stop drinking before you be too drunk before we get there. They might not let your ass in the club if you too drink "Raleigh said to Menijah as they passed a blunt around. " Yeah and your ass is not spoiling my night because I'll leave your ass right in the car until the club let out "said Zikhya. "Yeah and I'll throw up all in your shit too "slurred Menijah. " Yeah and I bet you I beat your ass too "said Zikhya looking in her rearview mirror at Menijah ready to pull over, drag her out the car, and beat her ass. Menijah just smacked her teeth and rolled her eyes. " Why this bitch always only get slick with me when she drunk? Thought Zikhya. She made a mental note to whip her ass if she kept asking for it. She loved Menijah, but she knew Menijah didn't want it with her. She pushed that thought to the back of her mind as she thought about her plans to get with Mo-T. She just hoped everything went as planned.

Private Stock on West Belvedere Avenue in West Baltimore was packed as the girls fought their way through the crowd. They were greeted with weed smoke and of course the stench of alcohol. Lil Wayne's Lollipop was blasting through the speakers and everybody was on the dance floor. When they walked through it was as if the guys were drooling over superstars. When they reached the bar, they ordered double shots of Dom Perignon. " It's jumping off in here!" Raleigh yelled over the music grinding in her seat. "I know!" yelled Menijah following suit. All of a sudden there was loud laughter near the front entrance and when Zikhya looked up she almost choked on her drink. " I be back!" she yelled to Raleigh as she almost knocked her off the stool trying to get up. " Damn Zikhya!" yelled Raleigh, but Zikhya was almost halfway to the bathroom. " What was that about?" asked Menijah. " Fuck if I know "said Raleigh, but as she looked toward the front entrance and saw the Mekhi Pheifer looking alike getting mad love from everybody in the spot, she knew what was up. "Shit Zikhya, get it together "she spoke to herself as she paced the floor. She was a nervous wreck as she feared her plans falling apart. She hadn't expected to see Mo-T at the same club se was in. She hadn't thought that far ahead. It was crazy how Mo-T made her feel when she saw him, like she second guessed her confidence in her appearance. She laughed looking in the mirror and shook her head thinking she was just nervous. Zikhya gave credit where it was due and she actually thought there were some very attractive females in the world, but she had to admit that she was a sexy, bad body, yellow bitch. As she continued to look at herself in the mirror, she thought about how her and Mo-T made a good couple. She loved Sequoia like a sister, but since that day on the cruise that Mo-T chose Sequoia over her, she promised herself that if she ever got the chance to throw the PP(Platinum Pussy) on Mo-T that she would lay it on his ass good! She made a exit back out to the club. "You cool bitch" Raleigh asked Zikhya when she came back to the bar. " Yeah, I need another drink "she said as she tried to wave down the busy bartender.

"I love that pose! Keep it right there! Lovely!" shouted the photographer as Sequoia did her thing. She didn't know where the confidence came from, but she felt like she was born to model. She thought that she would be nervous, but surprisingly she wasn't. " Cut!" . That word was like music to sequoia's ears. Although she had been having so much fun since she arrived, she was extremely tired. It was a lot of work, but the females on the cover made it look so easy. " Great job!" said the smiling photographer as he walked up to Sequoia. " Thank you Torez for being so patient with me "said Sequoia. " No, thank you, beautiful" said Torez looking into Sequoia's eyes. Torez quickly changed the subject as he handed Sequoia a Deer Park bottled water. "We have covered more than half of the shoots so all we have to do is send them to the CEO of VIBE magazine and see if he approves. So I'll be in touch. "said Torez. " Okay, great. Thanks again Torez "said Sequoia walking away heading back to her five star hotel suite. " Hey Sequoia "Torez called after her. Sequoia stopped in her tracks and turned to face Torez. " Wassup Torez", she asked. " You seem to be a girl who knocks at the door of opportunity when one presents itself, correct?" asked Torrez. " Well, yes but what is this all about?" asked Sequoia getting fustrated that he was beating around the bush. He saw her agitation and made it quick as he continued. " I'm a man with connections to many opportunities "said Torez handing Sequoia his business card as he disappeared. She was confused, but she dropped the card in her Coach purse and kept going. Torez was drop dead gorgeous, but she was in love with Morton. No man had changed that in nine years and she doubted if they could. As soon as she arrived in her suite, she dialed Mo-T's cell number. She missed her baby. "Wassup baby, workin hard?" Mo-T asked Sequoia. " Awwww man, baby you have no idea. Wassup with you though?" asked Sequoia frowning as he picked up on the loud music in the background. She instantly became angry at the thought of M-T waiting until she went out of town to have a house party with all his hoes. " You know I'm at Private Stock doing the norm, handling business. I miss you though" said Mo-T meaning every word. Sequoia knew what it was so she couldn't complain. Not to mention that the money he brought in was damn good. " I miss you too baby. It's only been two days since we've been apart and it feels like two decades "Sequoia whined. Just then Mo-T spotted Raleigh, Zikhya, and Menijah. " Them freak bitches just walked in here" laughed Mo-T. " Oh them bitches went to the After Hour and didn't tell me they were going? Put one of them bitches on telephone "said Sequoia a tad bit jealous. " You wasn't going anyway Sequoia. I told you that you not going be hanging with them bitches lie that, didn't I?" said Mo-T. " Baby I know so hush. I'm just saying they could have told me, now put one of them on the phone, please?" said Sequoia getting agitated with Mo-T. " Alright, hold on "said Mo-T as he waved Raleigh and Zikhya over who ere already looking in his direction. " Oh shit girl he want us to come over there!" said Raleigh excited. " Shut up and act cool!" said Zikhya poking Raleigh in her side with her elbow. "Damn she phat" thought Mo-T as he watched Zikhya strut toward him with Raleigh in tow. Menijah was too busy dancing with everything in the spot with a set of testicles. " Wassup "said Zikhya giving Mo-T dap. " Shit" said Mo-T. " Wassup boy!", said Raleigh about to give Mo-T dap, but he pulled his hand back. " Fuck you Mo-T. " Watch your mouth when you speaking to a grown man", said Mo-T. " Please "Raleigh said rolling he eyes and folding her arms across he chest. " Bring my phone over by the pool area when ya'll sluts done using it "said Mo-T walking away. " No he didn't", said Raleigh looking at Zikhya, but she was in a trance as he watched Mo-t bop back to the pool area. He might have offended Raleigh, but he turned her on in the worst way. Sequoia yelling hello through the phone brought her back to. " Oh, yeah I'm here. Wassup girl "said Zikhya. "Why ya'll bitches aint tell me ya'll was going to Private Stock "asked Sequoia. " We didn't know. We just got bored and decided to go. Wassup though? Is the photographer cute?" asked Zikhya. " Girl, you wouldn't believe his old sexy Italian ass trying to get fresh "laughed Sequoia. " Girl you lucky Mo-T not standing in earshot. Oh so he is cute?" smiled Zikhya hoping Sequoia fucked him and became sidetracked while she seduced Mo-T. " Girl, Im in love with Morton. I never cheated on my husband and I'm not about to start "Sequoia said confidently. She said that for nine years, but now was the only time she wasn't so sure of that. Torez had an aura about him that drew her to him when she first laid eyes on him; like an invisible magnet was on his somewhere pulling her in beyond her control. Not to mention the fact that he was very well connected, very financially secure, and a beautiful as the most gorgeous sunset you've ever seen. " I hear that. Well, I'll keep an eye on Mo-T for you. You know you my girl "said Zikhya. " Oh nobody's replacing me and aint no hoes getting my stacks. I have nine years experience with his ass. What bitch can top that?" said Sequoia. " You have no idea "thought Zikhya to herself. Tired of beating around the bush, Zikhya asked the question she really wanted to know the answer to. " So how long you think you going be staying down there?" " Well Torez said I'm done half of the shoots that VIBE requested. He sent them to the CEO and as soon as he hear something he's supposed to tell me. " Oh okay. Well I'm a go finish getting my drink on and please talk to Raleigh before I slap the shit out of her cause she staring all in my face "said Zikhya handing Raleigh the phone and walking back to the bar. " Wassup trick "said Raleigh. " Wassup Trick?" said Sequoia. " My ass in the air "said Raleigh and both girls burst into laughter. " Naw, but for real how u doing?" asked Raleigh. " I'm cool. Its a lot of work and I can't wait to get home "said Sequoia. "Well we watching your boo for you "said Raleigh. " Why do they keep saying that?" thought Sequoia. Just then her hotel phone rung. " Oh I forgot I was waiting for my photographer to call me back. Tell Mo-T I love him and I'll call him later" said Sequoia rushing off the phone. " Okay, love you bye "said Raleigh hanging up. She walked over to the pool area and gave Mo-T his phone. He didn't even look up at her when he took the phone out of her hand. She felt ignored and pouted as she made her way back to the bar with Zikhya.

Chapter Three

Zikhya was in deep though as she sat at the bar listening to T. I. 's Big Shit Poppin' blast through the speakers. In reality, she didn't know how deep Mo-T's love ran for Sequoia because she had heard of his many encounters of infidelity. How far would he go? She didn't want to approach him and get shot down, so she quickly came up with a plan. She walked over to the pool area where Mo-T was. " Hey mo-T can I speak to you for a minute "she asked walking off to the side out of the earshot of the pool players. "Wassup" . " Your boy ova there wearing that green and white fitted, wassup wit him. Mo-T laughed. " Forreal, Im trying to see what's good wit him", said Sequoia. " I got you. Let me go holler at him and let him know what's up real quick and we be back ova here "said Mo-T knowing all too well the game Zikhya was playing. If she thought she wanted to play those games with mo-T, she had the right opponent. When he was done with her she would begging for him smash her out. He told Sequoia to stop fucking with them hoes, maybe this would an opener once shit hit the fan. Knowing bitches, it would hit the fan sooner than he thought. He knew he would come out on top regardless because Sequoia wasn't going anywhere. " Alright, bet" said Zikhya. As soon as Mo-T was out of earshot, Raleigh put her two cents in. "Bitch what the fuck you doing?" . " Look bitch, Im fucking this cat, you hold the tail. Stop playing wit that drink and do something wit it "said Zikhya drowning her fifth double shot of Dom Perignon. " Don't get smart hoe "said Raleigh rolling her eyes at Zikhya. The two had taken turns keeping an eye on Menijah and from what they could see she was wasted. " Look at her "said Zikhya shaking her head. "You got to admit though, even drunk, that bitch look sexy "said Raleigh. " Of course, look who she roll wit "said Zikhya. " Point made "said Raleigh. Just then "Hate it or Love it" by Fifty Cent and The Game blasted through the speakers and the club went wild. " Oooh, this bear going through me, I'll

Zikhya looked up just in time to see two guys carrying Menijah to the rear exit of the club. She gulped the remaining of her drink down and rushed over to them. " Hold up, what the fuck is up!" she yelled over the music grabbing Menijah by the arm. She was buzzing and ready to fight a dude or a bitch, it was what it was. " Fucking is what's up and unless you game get the fuck out my way, bitch", said the slim, light skinned guy out of the two. The short darkskinned, clean cut one laughed. Zikhyya spit in the face of the slim one and before he could strike her Mo-T came out of nowhere. " We got a problem in this bitch motha fuckas!" yelled mo-T as he waved his two glocks in the air with his army of niggaz behind him. The two guys instantly held their hands up in the air. " No trouble son. Come on Butch let's bounce "said the shorter guy. " I'll be seeing you again "smiled the light skinned guy. " I wouldn't be so sure of that bitch boy "Zikhya smirked as she nodded her head toward the two glocks Mo-T still had pointed toward them. " We'll see" He said as him and his boy made an exit. " What was that all about?" asked his homeboy wearing the green and white fitted. " Tell you later. Right now, Zikhya this Nook, Nook this my wife home girl Zikhya "said Mo-T putting his guns back in their holsters on his hip. " My niggaz don't buy drinks, they buy bottles, so whatever you want he got you. Im going back to playing pool "said Mo-T as he bopped of feeling nice from the Tequila he was drinking. " Hold up Mo-T, let me take Menijah home and I'll be back. She drunk and she look like she bout to hurl" Mo-T must have been drunker than he thought because all of a sudden all he could think about was Zikhya's lips wrapped around his dick. However, he still remained under control. " Naw, you stay here with Nook, me and my nigga Tate will take her "said Mo-T waving Tate over. Tate was a short cute mothafucka. Zikhya thought it was cute how everybody in their crew had to be about five foot seven and under. No matter how cute Tate was, Zikhya had her eye on Mo-T fo sho!" Who are you" said Raleigh looking Tate up and down licking her lips. " This Tate, Tate this my wife other home girl Raleigh. We be back though, we taking Menijah home "said Mo-T holding the right side of Menijah. " Yo and I think shorty pissed on herself "said Tate frowning holding the left side of Menijah. She was so out of it, but she made progress as she stumbled to keep up with Tate and Mo-T. Zikhya and Raleigh were so mad at her they didn't even look at her. They knew she was going to get like that that's why they told her to stop drinking on the way to the club. They hated seeing her like that, but it was what it was. " Alright Mo-T get her home safe and I'll see ya'll when ya'll get back. Here go my house keys" said Zikhya handing Mo-T the keys. " Hurry and get him back here" said Raleigh eye balling Tate. " Keep your panties on girl, we be back!" yelled Mo-T as him and Tate exited the club.

"Damn shorty still passed out "said Tate as him and Mo-T made it backdownstairs. Mo-T had Tate take Menijah's clothes off and just put her under the comforter in her room with the door shut as he stood in the hall and waited for him. " I'm getting something to drink real quick then we can bounce "said Mo-T opening up Zikhya's refrigerator. " This bitch got a T. V. built into her refrigerator, for what? Bitches always go overborad" said Mo-T shaking his head. " Her place is laid though son "said Tate drowning his Arizona Iced Tea. " I'm taking this Chanel perfume, she beat for this so I can spray my Escalade because of her funky ass friend" said Mo-T. " Yo look at this digital camera. This bitch gangsta" said Tate handing it over to Mo-T. " Yeah, it's a camcorder built in it too" said Mo-T. " Man I got to take a leak then I'll be ready. Where's a bathroom at besides all the way back up them fucking steps "said Tate. "It's one through the kitchen behind the spiral staircase "said Mo-T. As soon as Tate vanished, Mo-T went through the silver digital camera and couldn't believe what he saw. Not only did he see explicit photos of Menijah, Raleigh, and Zikhya, but also of Sequoia. " I'm going to fuck her up "he thought to himself as he deleted them. Out of curiousity, he pressed play when it was in camcorder mode and almost dropped the camera at the sight before him. Zikhya was dressed in a sheer fully laced lingerie and sexy red pumps with a silver steel heel. She was entertaining the camera as she rubbed all over herself. She pinched her nipples proceeding to push her breast together, push them up towards her mouth, and suck them. " Damn" thought Mo-T as he felt his dick getting hard. What he saw next, once again blew his mind. With Zikhya, the surprises just didn't stop. " OOOh ...Mo-T.... fuck this pretty pink pussy.... oooh yeeah " moaned Zikhya fingering herself wildly as she fantasized about Mo-T. She quickened her pace plucking an =d smacking her clique as she spread her thick yellow leas wide apart. She laid back on her bed and whoever was filming got a close up on her wide open pussy dripping cum as she reached her orgasm. "You ready?" asked Tate startling Mo-T. Mo-T quickly put the camera on the computer stand. " Let's be out son "he said as he grabbed both sets of keys and he and Tate headed out the door.

"What the fuck is taking them so long? asked Raleigh. " Girl calm down, Tate coming "laughed Zikhya. " Well I'm going to dance "said Raleigh dancing her was to the dance floor. Zikhya and Nook sat and talked about any and everything. She was surprised at how comfortable she felt around him. Nook wasn't pressed and he made it known because his phone had been blowing up since he sat down to talk to her. " Your phone been blowing up. Them hoes on you like that? They must don't have no pride about theirself" said Zikhya taking another sip out of her bottle of Cristal. " Naw shorty it aint like that, it's mostly business "said Nook licking his lips. " What you know about that "laughed Zikhya. " You real funny "said Nook. The vibe Zikhya got from Nook was more of a brother and sister type thing. All of a sudden she had second thoughts about being with Mo-T. Sequoia was like a sister to her and they had been going strong together for a long time. However, she felt betrayal was worth having Mo-T, even if she couldn't have him permanently. " There they go right there "said Nook looking at Mo-T and Tate laughing as they came through the door. " What's so funny?" asked Zikhya squinting her eyes at Mo-T. " Nothing man chill out. Ya girl good. Aye, yo let's go back to my crib cause the crowd getting a gap in it forreal" said Mo-T throwing Zikhya her keys. " That's wassup. Tate go get Raleigh for me" said Zikhya.

Nook rode with Zikhya and they both were drunk talking shit to each other. He reminded her so much of her brother. From that point on, she knew they couldn't be anything more than friends. Tate rode shotgun as Mo-T drove and Raleigh sat in the backseat thinking she could sing. She was singing Keyshia Cole's "Love" and she sounded horrible. " Sequoia must have put that bullshit in "said Mo-T pulling in the driveway of their home. Zikhya pulled in beside him. Once everybody was out of the garage, Mo -T pushed a button on a small remote and the garage doors shut horizontally. He put the remote in the back pocket of his Red Monkey jeans and headed to the side door as everyone followed closely behind him. The sensors lights came on immediately, courteously of Sequoia. When they were all settled in the house, Mo-T reset the security alarm and him and Tate headed over to the built-in Wet Bar. " Ya'll want something?" Mo-T asked Zikhya and Raleigh. " What ya'll get?" asked Zikhya making her way to the bar as her heels clicked on the gorgeous floor. " You know what we do, Henny all day "said Mo-T leaving Nook and zikhya at the bar walking into the living room towards his surround sound stereo system with is drink in his hand paying Tupac's "Aint Nothing but a Gangsta Party" . " That's my shit!" yelled Raleigh grinding her ass on Tate and he enjoyed it. Nook was on his phone sounding as if he was negotiating a sale. Zikhya watched Mo-T from where she stood at the bar as he took off his Red Monkey T-shirt wearing only his beater. " " Damn", she thought as in between her legs became soaked. Mo-T's large firm back was revealed and every time he moved, his muscles flexed. On top of that, he was sweaty. Raleigh saw Zikhya eyeing Mo-T and walked over to her. " I see you looking bitch. What you waiting on? This is the perfect opportunity "she said drowning the last of her Grey Goose. " I do things different from you Raleigh. Mo-T is going to chase me "said Zikhya as she watched Mo-T sit on the double threaded plush bopping his head to Tupac and laughing with Tate and Nook. As always, Raleigh walked over to them and said something. " What ya'll laughing at?" she asked as he switched extra hard and put her hands on her hip. Zikhya knew she just wanted Mo-T to se her, but when you want to be seen by a guy that's not how you go about it. Zikhya decided to let Raleigh make herself look like a fool. Out of nowhere, Tate stuck his tongue down her throat and led her down the basement. " Damn they didn't waste any time did they?" said Zikhya wishing Mo-T would rip her clothes off and fuck her right where she stood. " He's playing the game like me. I can't let him win "thought Zikhya. " Ya'll want to smoke?" asked Mo-T. " I'm game "said Zikhya and Nook. The trio laughed, drink, smoked and laughed some more. Soon Nook was knocked out next to Zikhya. " Now is the perfect time to take advantage of him "laughed Mo-T from the other side of the room laying in his back on the floor. " You wild", laughed Zikhya feeling her pussy throbbing. " Well it's Tuesday, like three in the morning and I know my wife sound asleep. Let me make a phone call real quick and bounce . I'm sure ya'll can use some privacy "said Mo-T getting up off the floor heading to the Wet Bar to retrieve his Sidekick. " I hate him!" Zikhya thought. She had a choice. She could either let Mo-T walk away and miss out on a possibly one time opportunity to get the fuck of her life by a man she had been lusting after for nine years and save her friendship with Sequoia or get that monkey off her back and satisfy her purring kitten.

You look absolutely stunning if I must say so myself" said Torez looking across the table at Sequoia. " Thank you Torez. You look mighty handsome yourself "smiled Sequoia. " What do you think about me?" asked Torez as he took a sip from his champagne. Zikhya quickly grabbed her glass, gulped it down and waved a waiter over to get more. Back at the hotel when Torez called while she was on the phone with Zikhya, Torez requested a late dinner date with Sequoia. When she asked why so late, he said he wanted the mood to be intimate. Not knowing how to respond, Sequoia agreed figuring it wouldn't hurt just to have dinner. In reality she was attracted to Torez and thought it would be stepping into a trap if she had dinner with him. However, she went against her better judgment. She didn't know why, but she went all out with her appearance. It shocked her because she only did that for Mo-T. She secured her long hair in two bobby pins to the right side and curled the bottom. The curls fell beautifully down to the nape of her cleavage. To say her make-up was flawless would be an understatement. Her lips were sexy and shiny and she smelled of Red Door perfume. She wore a elegant red Dolce and Gabana wrap around dress with aqua trimming on the seams complimented by her red and aqua J-Lo baby doll high heels. Torez laughed at her nervousness. " You don't have to answer right now. Come on, let me show you something "said Torez taking Sequoia by the hand. The champagne had kicked in and she just went with the flow. She was living in that moment and for the first time in years, she wasn't thinking about Mo-T. It wasn't that Mo-T didn't provide her with the finer things in life, but it was taking the time out to whine and dine her that he lacked because of his dedication to the streets. How could she have known that what she yearned for so much from Mo-T would be in her photographer>Their destination was The Crystal Physique. The outside of the building looked like a castle and the inside was breathtaking. Simply put, it was something out of a fairytale. The ride on the elevator seemed to take forever, but when they reached their suite, Sequoia realized that the ride was well worth it. Torez led her to a balcony over looking the entire city of Las Vegas. It was the most mind relaxing view Sequoia had ever saw in her life. It was so romantic and definitely a place to come to and clear your head. She felt that she could stay there forever. The fresh air was crisp and the breeze felt like heaven. " Nice, isn't it? asked Torez. " Oh Torez could stay here forever "said Sequoia through glassy eyes. " You know it doesn't have to end "said Torez walking closer to Sequoia . As she felt Torez breath on her neck, she closed her eyes. She had allowed herself to get back into a corner and now there was nowhere to run. She grabbed Torez by his long silky black hair and kissed him hard and passionately. He picked her up and carried her to the bed in the suite. Sequoia then did something she never did since she had been married to Morton Wallace: She gave herself to Torez; all of her,

Chapter Four

"So you determined to win this little game we both playing, huh Mo-T?" Zikhya asked Mo-T as she got off the couch and stood directly in front of him looking in his eyes. " I don't know what you talking about shorty "laughed Mo-T still trying to get past Zikhya to go out the door. " You know what, game over "said Zikhya grabbing Mo-T's Akademik hoodie by both hands and pulling him to her. " Say it then "said Mo-T. " Fuck me" said Zikhya jumping into Mo-T's arms and wrapping her legs around his waist. The alcohol and weed had totally taken control of the both of them. " Yeah bitch that's what I want to hear. I been watching this phat ass all night and you know it don't you?" Mo-t asked Zikhya as he laid her on the couch and ripped her clothes off. Zikhya couldn't respond because her mouth was buried in Mo-T's neck. They went at one another like animals. Mo-T buried is face between her legs sucking and nibbling on her pussy like a hungry bear. Mo-T may have cheated on his wife, but never in the entire nine years had he put his head between another woman's thighs besides his wife, until now. At that moment Sequoia was the farthest thing from his mind. He was enjoying the way Zikhya tasted. " Mmmm, I knew this pussy tasted good "moaned Mo-T as Zikhya mashed his face in her pussy. " Ohhhh... Mo-T what you doing to me "moaned Zikhya. It was everything she thought it would be. Now she knew why Sequoia was on the hush about their sex life. Not using protection, when Mo-T entered Zikhya, she gasped. He was huge and she had to get used to him. After she adapted to the pain, they moved to a rhythm. The pain was still there but it was bearable. The sweat dripping down his back and his moaning turned Zikhya on so much that she lost count of how many times she reached her climax. At that moment when Mo-T was inside of her Zikhya knew she couldn't just be with him only once. Now that Zikhya had gotten a taste of Mo-T, she planned on keeping him around. She hadn't expected to get so attatched after being physical with him, but now it was too late. She had made up her mind to be prepared for battle when Sequoia came home;even if it meant loosing her friendship.

Sequoia was back at her hotel suite taking a shower and she couldn't stop crying. Just then, her cell phone started ringing. " Menijah? Why the hell she keep calling me so many times?" thought Sequoia. She was too upset to answer, so she ignored the calls. She felt so guilty about what she had done. Torez didn't treat her any differently than he had before they had sex than he did after. In fact, he was getting very much attached to Sequoia. She woke up to a room full of flowers and breakfast in bed. She had to admit that she loved the way Torez took time out to please a woman. All women want to feel special and Torez knew exactly how to make that possible. None the less, it was wrong because she was very well a married woman, but she was so confused. After she got out of the shower, she went into a deep sleep. Four hours later, she was awakened by her ringing Blackberry Storm on the nightstand. She looked at the time. " Damn, I slept that late?" . She looked at the caller ID and saw Mo-T's number flashing on the screen. She bit her lip to stop from crying, took a deep breath, and answered. " Hey baby?" said Sequoia. "Tell me what's wrong with you right now Sequoia "said Mo-T seriously. He knew his wife so well, he heard it in her voice. " Mo-T I'm fine. " Why didn't I hear from you al day?" Mo-T asked. " Baby because I'm exhausted and I just woke up "said Sequoia yawning. " You better be tired from working and nothing else "said Mo-T seriously. " Okay, you know what…. . " " I'm sorry ma, my bad. You know how I am about you" said Mo-T. Mo-T's guilt for what he had done with Zikhya was eating at him, but not enough for him to stop. " Yeah baby, I know" . " Did your sidekicks call you yet?" asked Mo-T curiously. " Menijah kept calling me, but I didn't answer because I was tired. "said Sequoia. " Why she call you instead of Raleigh or Zikhya?" asked Mo-T playing it off. " I don't know, but I'll call her back to see what's up because she did keep calling like something was wrong "said Sequoia. " Alright baby. Wel I know you got to go, so I'm not going to hold you up. Call me the very first chance you get "said Mo-T. " Okay babe, I love you, bye" said Sequoia hanging up.

"Damn, ya'll just don't know!" yelled Mo-T grabbing at himself as he took one last pull of the blunt and passed it to Nook. Mo-T, Nook, and Tate were all at the park getting wasted. Each of them had a story to tell and Mo-T was up first. "Yo, I know it wasn't that good to the point where that bitch going be taking shorty place. Shit, Sequoia is straight class man and Zikhya is no competition. " said Nook. Don't get it wrong, Nook liked Zikhya a lot and looked at her as a little sister. However, the truth was the truth; she was a slut and nowhere near wifey material. "Fuck no, nigga!" yelled Mo-T.

" She cool peoples though, but shorty definitely a freak. My cousin Ghost hit her under the bridge one night after the club "said Tate. "Yeah nigga and I know you didn't eat that trashy pussy nigga "said Nook Mo-T's silence told them everything they needed to know. " Awww, come on man! What fuckin' part of the game is that?" asked Tate. " Yo, you fuckin' up big time and I just want to let you know that. You don't know where the fuck that hoe been!" yelled Nook. " Oh, hell no! Hold the fuck up Mo-T, I know you used a condom on that dirty bitch, please tell me you did?" pleaded Tate. " Hold the fuck up, do I look like a fuckin' child to either one of ya'll!?" yelled Mo-T. " Ya'll want to know the truth, I didn't use shit with her!" yelled Mo-T looking at his friends. " It's a lot that could come from that, are you ready for it? asked Nook. " I was born ready motha fuckas!" yelled Mo-T. Let me ask you something yo. Sequoia is not just some tramp you met and picked up at the club man, she's your wife. You mean to tell me that you don't feel just a tad bit of guilt for fucking her home girls?" asked Tate. " Man, it's like this. Those bitches are beneath my wife and always will be. I'm a fuckin'man and I must admit that all the bitches got a nice frame on them. Zikhya stand out cause for one, she's red and I love red bones yo. Something about them just turns me all the way the fuck on. I still got sense though, what the fuck can them hood rat bitches do for me? My wife held me down on a lot of shit and I got to give her mad respect for that. At the same time, my wife is the type of person where if you tell her something, she has to find out if it's true on her own. All I was trying to do was open her eyes and let her know that bitches and niggas are two different species. A nigga can tell another nigga that his girl not shit and the niggas can set her up to get caught. The best part of it all is them two niggas goin' still remain friends and say fuck that hoe, they not goin' beef with each other. They goin' try to fuck that hoe together and then pass her around to whoever else want her. Ya dig? said Mo-T. " Shit, well since you sharing nigga, can I hit that good motha fucka?" asked Tate. The trio laughed. " Shit, why not? It's no fun if the homies can't have none!" laughed Mo-T as he gave Tate and Nook high fives.

"Girl, it was off the chain!" yelled Zikhya falling back on her bed. She and Raleigh were in her bedroom sitting on her bed Indian style smoking a blunt. Zikhya was filling Raleigh in on all the events that transpired the night her and Mo-T had sex. " Girl, I'm going have to get me some of that "said Raleigh. " Bitch you lucky you my girl cause I definitely wouldn't share that otherwise. " So let's fuck him together "said

Raleigh passing the blunt back to Zikhya. " Alright, we can do that tonight then, I'm sure he game "said Zikhya. Meanwhile, Menijah was on her way to the bathroom and heard their whole conversation; they thought she was still sleep. " Yo, where was Nook at though "asked Raleigh. " Girl his ass was snoring like a new born baby!" laughed Zikhya. " Ya'll nasty; how ya'll going fuck right next to that man "laughed Raleigh. " Shit, girl he probably wanted a piece. " So would you let him in on a foursome?" asked Raleigh ready for some action. " Girl, hell naw! He's like a brother to me. You wouldn't believe how much he reminds me of Zonado "said Zikhya. " For real?" Raleigh said shocked. Zikhya hadn't spoken about her brother for a while because she kept all her feelings bottled up inside. Every since he died, Zikhya knew she was on her own and she felt so alone until she met her girls Menijah, Sequoia, and Raleigh. Although Zikhya would be getting checks from her mother and her brother's death for the rest of her life, she still put some money away in a safe for a rainy day. "Come on girl, let's hit up Victoria Secret in Arundel Mills Mall and get ready for tonight "said Zikhya jumping off the bed getting dressed. " On you "asked Raleigh. " Isn't it always? "Raleigh rolled her eyes at Zikhya leaving out her room to go to her own and get dressed. " I'm just fucking wit you "laughed Zikhya. " Whatever bitch!" yelled Raleigh slamming her door. " Wassup Menijah, you want to go with us?" asked Zikhya. " Where ya'll sluts going?" asked Menijah with her towel wrapped around her body. "Victoria Secret "said Zikhya. " Naw, I'm cool. Girl, I still have a hangover from lastnight. Where were ya'll bitches at last night anyway? Asked Menijah not wanting Zikhya to know she already knew. " None-ya!" laughed Zikhya knocking on Raleigh's bedroom door as she stood in the hallway talking to Menijah. " Whatever "said Menijah walking past Zikhya to her room and shutting the door. " I'm ready. Let's roll "said Raleigh putting her Juicy Couture shades on and following Zikhya downstairs and out the door. Not once did Zikhya was so stuck on having bragging rights that she not once thought about the health of herself, knowing that Mo-T's infidelities were no secret.

Menijah had just started lotioning her legs with Pomegranate scented body rub when she heard a knock on the door. She ignored it, figuring it was Zikhya and Raleigh forgetting something. After the knocking didn't stop, she became agitated. "Use your fucking key Zik…. . " She stopped in mid sentence when she saw Mo-T standing on the other side of the door as she swung it open wildly with her towel still on. "I don't have a key and is Zikhya here?" asked Mo-T. " No, her and Raleigh went to Arundel

Mills. You just missed them "said Menijah feeling uncomfortable because she was standing in front of Mo-T with a towel on. " I got a couple of sales waiting for me so I really came over here to bag my shit up. Can I come in?" asked Mo-T. " Ummm, yeah" said Menijah moving aside to let Mo-T in. He went straight to the kitchen and pulled out his large Ziploc bag of weed. His phone was blowing up. " I said I got you man! Damn, give me at least ten minutes! "yelled Mo-T to one of his customers, "I'll be upstairs if you need anything "said Menijah. That's wassup" said Mo-T not looking up from the table. Menijah shut her bedroom door behind her and walked to her closet to pick out what she was going to wear for the day. When she turned around to lay it out on the bed, Mo-T was standing right behind her naked. " Oh shit!" she tried to cover up her body, but it was no use. Mo-T kissed her roughly and laid her down on the bed spreading her legs . He sucked her big nipples roughly and the pain felt so good. "Mmmmmm…. " she moaned. "Your hair is so pretty "he whispered in her ear rubbing his fingers through her hair. " Fuck me "Menijah moaned lifting her legs up and wrapping them around his waist. " You want me to fuck this good Indian pussy? I know it's good "said Mo-T. As he, once again without protection, entered her and pounded her roughly, Menijah was speechless. " Look at that big ass jiggling girl "said Mo-T as he flipped her over and fucked her from the back. She could barely catch her breath because Mo-T was so thick and big, filling up her whole pussy. Mo-T sat on a chair and positioned Menijah on top of him as she rode him like a stallion. " Bend over and touch your toes without bending your knees" . Menorah did as she was told. She never had a dick like that before. "I'm about to cum!" she yelled as her thick thighs started shaking uncontrollably. "Squirt on that wood, I'm right behind you" said Mo-T as he pulled out of her and squirted cum on her back and hair. Just like that, he was gone without saying a word. Never in a million years would she have thought she would be sleeping with her best friend's husband, but some things are unexplainable. .

"Hello?" "Good afternoon beautiful", Torrez greeted Sequoia. He was so sweet. Those days with Mo-T were so long gone; Mo-T had married her and got too comfortable. " Good afternoon Torez" "How did you sleep?" . " Pretty good. " "How about we go for a ride on my yacht after we finish shooting today?" asked Torez. " Torez, we need to talk…" "Okay whatever it is we can discuss it on our wonderful boat ride. I'll see you then and wear something sexy "said Torez hanging up. " He is so determined "thought Sequoia as she looked at the dead phone line. She had to admit the aggression turned her on. She hung up the phone to give Menijah a call before she headed out for the day, but she kept getting her voicemail. She decided to leave a message. For some reason, Zikhya began to get a very uneasy feeling in the pit of her stomach. " Menijah this is me returning your calls. I hope everything is okay. Call me when you get this. Love you sis, bye" . It was strange to Sequoia that Menijah called her several times, but didn't answer when she called her back. Out of the four girls, Menijah was the one who was very thorough at returning telephone calls. She hoped that everything was okay back home as she proceeded to get ready for her day with Torez.

Menijah sat on her bed looking at the phone. She couldn't dare answer that phone knowing what she had just done to Sequoia. She couldn't believe she just had sex with her best friend's husband. Menijah knew that because of the type of per son she was, she had to tell Sequoia. She didn't know what type of friends Zikhya and Raleigh were, but she knew her love ran deep for Sequoia. She had made a mistake and now she had to pay for it. Things just happened so fast, she didn't even know how she didn't hear Mo-T come in her room. Temptation took over her and she gave in. She had to admit that it was the best sex she had ever had. No man had ever sexed her the way Mo-T did and she felt very bad for liking it. She felt dirty all over again and took another shower. She scrubbed herself in the scorching hot water, but it was to no avail. After she got out the shower, she sat on her bed with her head buried in a pillow and cried. "Menijah, we got you som…. " Zikhya and Raleigh stopped in mid sentence as they opened Menijah's door and saw her crying like a baby. " What's wrong Menijah?" Raleigh and Zikhya asked sitting on her bed rubbing her back. Menijah didn't respond. "What happened?" asked Raleigh. " Come on Menijah talk to us "said Zikhya. Still, Menijah said nothing. "You don't feel like talking?" asked Raleigh. Menijah was silent as she continued to cry. " Well when you ready to talk, we'll be in my room okay "said Zikhya getting up from Menijah's bed telling Raleigh to come on. As soon as they reached the door, Menijah spoke. " I fucked Mo-T and I know ya'll did too "said Menijah looking up at Raleigh and Menijah. They dropped their bags and their mouths hung open. "I heard ya'll conversation earlier when ya'll thought? I was sleep "said Menijah. " When the fuck did this take place?" asked Zikyha angry. " Zikhya, stop acting like he's your man "said Menijah. " Bitch he is my man while Sequoia gone, hit! I'm about to start evicting motha fuckas!" said Zikhya stomping out of Menijah's room as she went into her own room and slammed the door. " Menijah, how was it?" smiled Raleigh sitting back down next to Menijah. Menijah stopped crying and laughed. Raleigh always tried to make good out of a bad situation. " It was good "said Menijah. " Damn! That's what I heard "said Raleigh getting excited. "Well, me and Zikhya suppose to be fucking him together tonight and if you want to come, you can "said Raleigh. " Shit, I'm game "said Menijah. " " You phony bitch, on your bed crying like a punk" laughed Raleigh falling on the floor. " Fuck you "laughed Menijah kicking her while she was on the floor. "You don't feel bad about what you did to Sequoia?" asked Menijah. " **Shit, bitch we can share**!"

"You're pretty quiet tonight", said Torez. " Torez, I…" Sequoia didn't get a chance to finish. He started undressing her right there on his yacht. Sequoia wanted to stop him, but she just couldn't. He kissed her body from head to toe, "Stay right here, I have a surprise for you", said Torez going into another room on the yacht. Sequoia moved her body to Sade's "No Ordinary Love" as she waited for Torez to return. Seconds later he came back holding rose petals, body oil, and a bowl full of sliced chocolate covered strawberries. He walked over to Sequoia and admired her body. He stood over top of her and poured the warm oil from her neck all the way down to her feet. " Mmmmmm, that feels so good "moaned Sequoia. He knelt down beside her on his knees and began to massage her feet. He then worked his way up to her breast. He kissed her neck gently and then her lips. Torez grabbed the bowl of strawberries and fed them to her one by one. When he got to the last two strawberries, he one on each breast and sucked them off. Sequoia moaned in ecstasy . Then came the rose petals. Torez took a handful of them and sprinkled them all over her body. They stuck to her because of the oil and it was a beautiful sight to behold. " You look like a rose garden goddess "smiled Torez. The two made love in the candle lit scene as Sade played softly in the background. Sequoia was once again letting Torez explore her scared temple.

Chapter Five

"Tate, can I smoke wit you? Damn!" joked Raleigh. Zikhya, Nook, and Mo-T laughed as Tate passed the blunt. They were all back at the Embassy Suite hotel on Nursery Road having a ball. They had weed, drink by the gallons, and money. Mo-T was the D. J. blasting the music, of course Tupac. Menijah decided against going and stayed home to let what happened with her and Mo-T sink in. She was fighting a battle of whether she should be a true friend to Sequoia and tell her what happened behind her back or stay true to Raleigh and Zikhya and keep quiet. "I'm fucked up "said Zikhya smiling at Raleigh through slit eye lids. " Me too bitch" said Raleigh and the girls both burst out laughing. Mo-T got up and cut the lights off. All you heard were clothes coming off in the dark and belts jingling as everybody got undressed. "Mmmmm, bring that dick over here Mo-T" said Raleigh. Zikhya got mad. " Mo-T?" she asked. " Chill out girl; let's just have fun "he told Zikhya. She folded her arms and turned her back to them. "Do this for me baby, please?" asked Mo-T as he kissed her. "Alright, but you better not cum until you get over here wit me" said Zikhya. Nobody in that hotel room went untouched. Nook and Tate was on Raleigh tag teaming her while she was on her knees. Nook stood in front of her getting his dick sucked while Tate fucked her from the back. " What the fuck is this, the good pussy crew. Damn!" said Tate as he pounded Raleigh. Then Mo-T, Nook and Tate were on Raleigh. Mo-T got his dick sucked while Nook fucked Raleigh in her ass and Tate fucked her pussy. Then Tate and Mo-T was on Zikhya while Nook pushed Raleigh's legs all the way back to her head and fucked her hard and long. Tate stood over Zikhya and dipped his dick in her mouth while Mo-T drilled her pussy once again. Soon Zikhya was on the floor with her mouth open waiting for Mo-T and Tate to explode in and they did; in her mouth, on her hair, and all over her tities. Raleigh followed suit awaiting Nook as he squirted in her eye and all over her hair. Soon everyone was passed out sleep. Of course Zikhya tried waking Mo-T up for round two, but when he didn't budge she instantly got upset. " Mo-T get your ass up, shit!" she yelled hitting him in his head. " Damn,

27

I'm tired man. Everybody else sleep so take your ass to sleep" said Mo-T turning his back to her on the hotel bad. "Well, let me suck my dick then "she said kissing all over him. Those must have been the magic words because Mo-T immediately rolled over on his back and folded his hands behind his head. "I should have known that would make you move wit your nasty ass self "said Zikhya agitated. Just shut up and put my dick in your mouth "said Mo-T pushing her head down and sliding his dick down her throat. Zikhya gagged, but kept going as Mo-T moaned in pleasure. Having Zikhya's mouth wrapped around his dick was a dream come true that he wanted to live in forever. In the nine years that he and Sequoia had been together, he had never met a female who could take him away from Sequoia. He didn't know what it was about Zikhya, but he was ready to start fuckin' wit her on the regular. He figured since she had been lusting after him for so long, she might be down for a nigga long term. He didn't care that his homeboys had fucked her, that was the past; they would always be his niggas for life. What he didn't know was that his charm didn't work on all females like it did with Sequoia. He failed to realize that Sequoia put up with his cheating because she played her life strictly by the bible, which is why she never cheated until she went to Las Vegas. He would find out soon enough that Zikhya Palmer didn't come from that breed.

"Hurry up and pick out a movie Raleigh, damn!" Zikhya yelled. "Zikhya, give her a chance. We've only been here for fifteen minutes "said Menijah. "Well, Im going to my car and call my boo Mo-T to waste time. Ya'll hoes going be till tomorrow anyway "said Zikhya waving them off. " That's all that bitch wanted to do anyway. Thats why she was rushing us", said Raleigh. " I know. It's crazy how she acting like her and Mo-T is a couple. You don't think he's going along with it, do you?", Menijah asked Raleigh. " I don't know girl, she has a way of making a person do anything she want. Even if you know its dead fuckin' wrong", said Raleigh holding her head down. " You feel bad about what you did to Sequoia, right?" asked Menijah. Raleigh was near tears. " Yeah, I mean I will admit that I was jealous when she and Mo-T got married. I wanted a man who would love me the way Mo-T loved Sequoia. It seems like Sequoia found him just like that, but it's taking me to go through a thousand men to find Mr. Right" said Raleigh. " Raleigh, Sequoia is paying a price by being with Mr. Right so fast too. At the same time, you are supposed to be happy for her if you are a real friend. Zikhya don't care about anybody but herself and when she wants something she doesn't let anything or anyone stand in her way. She don't care if anybody gets hurt in the process, including herself because its in her bloodline; that's how she is and she's not changing. You on the other hand are not. I always knew you were just following Zikhya because you were afraid of what she might think about you if you did the right thing. If your love runs that deep for Sequoia, and obviously it does, tell her Raleigh. " said Menijah. Raleigh wiped the tears from her face. "I can't look her in her face and tell her that yo" said Raleigh starting to cry all over again. " Okay, look, we'll figure something out. Let's just go pick out a movie before Zikhya come in here yelling at us in front of the whole store. " said Menijah. Just then, they heard a commotion outside in the front of the store in the parking lot. "Bitch so the fuck what, what you mad because you didn't get him?" Zikhya yelled at the Indian looking girl with the long silky auburn hair. " Bitch I don't want his trifling ass. I just hate cruddy bitches like you. How the fuck you going be in Sequoia's face and be fucking her husband! You're a nasty bitch!" yelled the girl. "Well Tate sure doesn't seem to think so, bitch!" Just then Raleigh and Menijah realized that when the girl came from behind her car with a box cutter in her hand, she was pregnant. Raleigh rushed towards the girl to try to take the box cutter from her. "Zikhya take your ass back over to your car and get the fuck out of here before the manager in Blockbuster call the police!" yelled Menijah. " Naw, fuck that! That bitch think she going get tough with me, I don't give a fuck if she's pregnant. I'm going give that whore the business and show her what the fuck ids really up. Pregnant bitches get it too!" yelled Zikhya pushing Menijah on the ground. Menijah had to admit, the bitch was strong. " Zikhya stop! She got a box cutter and she's pregnant!" yelled Raleigh as she continued to hold the Indian girl back. " Bitch I swear if my name not Coa-Coa, I'm going beat the brakes off your motha fuckin' ass! You fucking somebody's baby father and somebody's husband? How fucking low can you get?" yelled Coa-Coa, who they now knew was Tate's baby mother. She and Sequoia used to be cool until she told Sequoia she didn't like Zikhya. Sequoia was still cool with her, but she told Coa-Coa Zikhya was fam and from where she was from fam always came first. Coa-Coa understood that. One day at the mall, Sequoia was out with Menijah, Zikhya, and Raleigh. She saw Coa-Coa and she spoke to her. Coa-Coa spoke to Sequoia, Raleigh, and Menijah to be smart. "Bitch I don't give a fuck if you don't speak to me" said Zikhya. "Bitch I know, all you care about is what dick is going to be down your throat next" said Coa-Coa. " Bitch don't get your fuckin' wig split" said Zikhya walking up on Coa-Coa, but Sequoia stopped her. Zikhya was strong, but

Sequoia was her match. She obeyed Sequoia and stepped back. Every since then, it been on between the two. "Ask Tate, he would know!" yelled Zikhya adding more fuel to the fire. That did it, and Raleigh could no longer hold Coa-Coa back. Raleigh felt for the girl because she was pregnant, but she was not about to let her stab Zikhya. Coa-Coa ran up to Zikhya and started choking her so hard she was turning red. Zikhya some kind of way got a hold of her Coa-Coa's hair and with all her might slung her on the ground. "Yeah, bitch what happened to all that mouth now!" yelled Zikhya as she sat on top of Coa-Coa's chest and punched her in her face over and over again while Raleigh kicked her in her head. Coa-Coa was fighting back with all her might, but it was no use. Zikhya and Raleigh had the upper hand and they were using it to their advantage. Soon, they heard police sirens in the distance. "Oh shit! Zikhya come on!" yelled Raleigh as she dragged Zikhya to the car where Menijah was already waiting and spun out of the parking lot. A bleeding Coa-Coa struggled to get up off the ground as an officer offered his help and began questioning her. " You okay mam", asked the officer as he helped Coa-Coa off the ground. "I'm good; get your fucking hands off of me!" yelled Coa-Coa yanking out of the officer's grasp. " Mam, I'm trying to help you. Do you need medical attention? I see that you're pregnant" stated the officer. "Did I ask for your fucking help?" asked Coa-Coa sarcastically. "Do you have an idea who did this to you? asked the officer. " Naw, it happened too fast. I didn't get anything" lied Coa-Coa leaning up against her car trying to catch her breath. " Any pain mam?" asked the officer. " I'm cool "said Coa-Coa. " Okay, well I'm officer Mason and here's my card. If you remember anything, please don't hesitate to give me a call, okay?" asked officer Mason. " Aight, that's wassup" said Coa-Coa getting in her car. As she started her car up, the officer walked up to her window. " Oh yeah Mrs. …" "Nikola Harrison, but you can call me Coa-Coa" . "Okay, Mrs. Coa-Coa, one more thing" . " What's that Mr. Officer?" . "When we do catch the people who did this to you, because we will, do you want to press charges?" asked Officer Mason. Coa-Coa had to laugh. She was from the mean streets of New York and up there you handled beefs the hood way; not the pigs way. She despised cops because she was raped by one in New York one night leaving the Cotton Club. Every since then, she been like fuck cops. "Excuse me, did I say something funny?" asked Officer Mason obviously offended by Coa-Coa's laughing. "Naw, naw, you straight. You know what; I don't even know who did this to me so let's just call it a night. ", said Coa-Coa pulling out of the parking lot. "Oh by the way, I like your pants. They compliment your ass well!" Coa-Coa yelled at the cop out of the window as she drove off. "Stupid bitch", mumbled Officer Mason to himself as he got back in his car getting back to work.

"I can't believe that bitch thought she was going to pop shit to me and get away with that shit" said Zikhya smoking a blunt to calm her nerves. " Zikhya you took that shit too far "said Menijah. " Yeah cause when you saw that she was pregnant, you should have just walked away and got at her when she dropped the baby for real "said Raleigh taking the blunt from Zikhya. "Bitch you got a nerve to tell me that because you sure had no problem kicking that bitch in her head "said Zikhya. They all laughed. "Yeah bitch but when I heard them police sirens, I got the fuck up out of there. "said Raleigh. "Speaking of getting low, Menijah where the fuck were you when all this was going down?" Zikhya asked Menijah. " Ya'll bitches know I don't do no fighting. Shit, I'm a lover not a fighter" said Menijah taking the blunt from Raleigh. Raleigh and Zikhya looked at each other and burst out laughing. Menijah had to laugh herself. " Damn and we still didn't get a movie "said Zikhya. "Shit fuck it, ya'll want to play the Wii?" asked Zikhya. "I'm game!" yelled both Menijah and Raleigh. Menijah put the blunt out in the heart shaped ashtray that sat on Zikhya's bed. "I'm got first!" yelled Menijah as she got up and ran downstairs. " I got seconds!" yelled Raleigh running behind her. " Now, that bitch last!" laughed Raleigh and Menijah giving each other high fives. "Oh, I'm about to be first, second, and last when I put ya'll bitches out" said Zikhya. " Oh lord, Menijah. Here she go again with that bullshit" said Raleigh. " That's right bitch and give me the new remote and you take the fucked up one so you can throw them fucked up balls. " laughed Zikhya. " It don't matter because I'm nice with it for real" said Raleigh.

Sequoia lay awake staring at the ceiling o f the yacht. She was stuck between a rock and a hard place. She felt herself falling for Torez and in reality, knew there was nothing she could do about it. He had explored the most sacred part of her that was supposed to strictly be for her husband. For the first time in her life, she sat and thought about if she was really happy. Sequoia had always put Mo-T's happiness before her own, but it was because she was so deeply in love with her husband. Sometimes she wondered why she stayed through all of Mo-T's cheating and lies. She knew she was a bad bitch, she had brains, and if she really had to, she could make her own dough. She caught herself questioning things that she never had given second thoughts to before. One thing was did Mo-T even want her to have a sense of her own independence or did he want her to depend on him so he could have that over her head? Did Mo-T think that by him controlling all the finances it would give Sequoia reason to say she wasn't leaving? Did Mo-T cheat on her whenever he got ready because he thinks that she would accept it for the rest of her life to stay in a comfort zone? Until now, Sequoia never realized how important the questions were that she was asking herself. What was the craziest part of it all, was that now Sequoia was wondering if she even still in love with Mo-T. She looked over at Torez and smiled as she rubbed his head. She felt so content with him and she couldn't deny that in just a few days of knowing him, she had caught feelings. She felt like she had known Torez forever and that was very out of character for her. She hadn't even been that comfortable around Mo-T when they first met nine years ago. Maybe it was his aggression that made her nervous and turned her on all at the same time. Just then, her thoughts were interrupted by her ringing cell phone. "Hello?" "Hey it's me" . "Menijah, it's late, wassup?" asked Sequoia holding the sheet around her as she sat up in bed looking over at Torez. She was glad he was out cold. " Sequoia..." Menijah what is it, you're scaring me. "Baby, is everything okay?" asked Torez rubbing his eyes. She quickly put her hand over the phone. " Yes baby everything's well, just get back to sleep "said Sequoia. Menijah had thought and thought all night about telling Sequoia the truth. She came to the conclusion that she couldn't tell her that she slept with Mo-T because she knew it would hurt her too bad. Even though all the girls were close, it seemed as if Menijah was closer to Sequoia than she was to Raleigh and Zikhya and vise-versa. Zikhya and Raleigh were closer to each other than they were with Menijah and Sequoia. After the bowling game was finished, Raleigh and Zikhya went out on a date with Mo-T and Nook. They asked Menijah to join but she decided against it. She wanted the chance to have a head start in telling Sequoia what went down, even though for right now she was leaving herself out. She just hoped Zikhya didn't catch wind of it because if she did, Menijah knew she would let everything out regardless of whose feelings got hurt. "Who was that?" asked Menijah. " Oh. . . uhhh, that was security doing room check "lied Sequoia, but it sure didn't sound like security to Menijah. "Oh okay "said Menijah to play it off like she didn't here a guy In the background sounding as if he was laid right next to Sequoia. "Now what did you have to tell me?" asked Sequoia. "Oh, well I didn't want to be the one to deliver bad news, but Zikhya and Raleigh slept with Mo-T.

Chapter Six

"Tate, you could have fucked anybody else! Why did you have to fuck that dirty bitch?" yelled Coa-Coa storming in the house. Tate was playing Madden on the X Box 360 when she came storming in the house with a bloody nose and busted lip. Her clothes were dirty and disheveled. Thinking something might be wrong with the baby; he threw the game down and came running to her. "Coa-Coa, you don't feel any pain do you?" he asked rubbing her stomach. "Get the fuck off of me!" yelled Coa-Coa as she slapped his hands away. " I'm the fuckin father, I can't be concerned? You better stop with that fuckin attitude shit bitch; I told you this is not fuckin New York because I will slide your ass!" yelled Tate not meaning it. He just hated her mouth sometimes. " Fuck you motha fucka! I'm tired of you fuckin around on me, and then you had to fuck that dirty bitch Zikhya? That's a fuckin insult!" yelled Coa-Coa. "Who the fuck told u that?" asked Tate trying to figure out how his dirt leaked out. One thing he knew for sure was that Mo-T was his main man and he wouldn't do any bitch shit like rat him out to his girl. Zikhya, Menijah, and Coa-Coa didn't know his girl, or so he thought, and they didn't live in the same area as them so it was no way they could have told her. " Is that all the fuck you have to say Tate, all the fuck you want to know is who told me, huh?" yelled Coa-Coa. When she started speaking in her New York accent, Tate knew she was pissed and there was no calming her down. He had to play it cool so he could get to the source, the snitch. " Baby, Baby, shhhhhhhh. Okay baby, calm down" said Tate hugging her and not letting her go no matter how hard she tried to pull away. He kissed the top of her head and rubbed his hands through her hair, which always worked. Soon, she began to cry. " Tate, why? I cook for you, I clean, I don't go out to clubs anymore because you tell me not to, I do anything you tell me to do and don't give you lip, I gave you a child when you asked for one even though my dad was pissed at me and I helped you get on your feet when your family didn't even help you! Why the fuck do you keep doing this to me?" cried Coa-Coa. Someone was trying to fuck up his home and take him away from his unborn seed and he wasn't having it. Whoever ratted him out would have to pay, big time. " Okay baby. Tell me who did this to your face so I can take care of it" said Tate. " You don't take care of shit! I'm going to take care of shit my own way! Your little girlfriend Zikhya and her girl Raleigh think this shit is over; well this shit is far from fuckin over! I got a trick for those bitches. " yelled Coa-Coa. Zikhya!" yelled Tate. " Yeeees, your little fuckin girlfriend. I saw her walking to her car and I stopped and pulled my shit over to let her know that she was a trifling ass bitch to be all up in Sequoia's face and be fucking her husband behind her back" said Coa-Coa. "Baby, you don't have anything to do with that! Why the fuck you doing dumb shit while you pregnant with my fuckin seed yo? I swear to God Coa-Coa if something happen to my baby, I'm going kill you. That's my word!" yelled Tate poking Coa-Coa in her head. " Fuck you Tate! You and your girlfriend. She made sure she told me all the details about you and her fucking the other night!" yelled Coa-Coa smacking his hand away. " Zikhya! Oh that bitch want to play games with me? I'm about to show her fuckin ass!" yelled Tate as he grabbed the keys to Coa-Coa Benz and headed for the door. Tate, I said I want to handle things my own way, where are you going?!" Coa-Coa yelled out the door at him. He ignored her. " Timothy Gray, you get your ass back here right fucking now!" "Bitch you want to fuckin play with me? Alright bitch, let me tell your stupid ass to get back in the house one more time and see what the fuck happen!" yelled Tate standing on the lawn looking up at Coa-Coa through red eyes as she stuck her head out the door. He didn't know why Coa-Coa was trying his patience because she knew that when his eyes turned like that to leave him the fuck alone. He could calm her down when she was upset when nobody else could, not even her parents. Coa-Coa knew that when Tate was mad, she couldn't do the same with him. She had a temper, but his was way worst than hers. For some reason she felt like trying him this day. "I'm not going no fuckin where!" yelled Coa-Coa looking at Tate rolling her eyes and moving her head with her hands on her hips. "Oh you think you crazy now bitch, I'm going show you who crazy!" yelled Tate as he started running up the front porch steps. Before he even hit the second step, Coa-Coa ran in the house and shut the door. " That's what I thought bitch!" yelled Tate as he walked back to her car. " Fuck you motha fucka, I'm not scared of you!" yelled Coa-Coa through the window. "Stop playing with me bitch! Stop fuckin playing with me alright!" Tate yelled at Coa-Coa through the window. Coa-Coa kept yelling at Tate, but he didn't pay her any mind. He spun out of the driveway headed to Mo-T's house where he knew Zikhya was because he talked to Mo-T not too long ago. They were talking about the night at the Embassy Suites hotel. Those bitches was playing like everything was cool, when they knew they had banked his baby mother. Hell no, Tate was having that. If he wasn't going smack all three of them bitches, his name wasn't Timothy Gray. He didn't give a fuck if Menijah wasn't included, he was slapping that bitch too just because she their home girl. He knew fucking with them scandalous bitches was trouble and he wished he never did. Sequoia was the only one he fucked with out their whole crew. Tate didn't understand Mo-T, why would he start fucking with a low-life ghetto ass bitch when he had a classy wife with a mean ass body? He was sure Sequoia's pussy wasn't garbage because Mo-T wouldn't have married her. The house was always clean when he came over and he knew damn well Mo-T wasn't cleaning it. He was in the streets with him from sun up till sun down. Sequoia go upstairs in their bedroom and shut her door when Mo-T have company and she cover herself up when company come around. Mo-T always told Sequoia that when he ate, his whole crew ate. There were no questions asked, Sequoia did as she was told. Shit there were times when a good hot meal was what a nigga needed for real and Sequoia always came through. The food would always be ready when they got there from being out all night. As a matter of fact, Tate never even heard Sequoia argue at him for staying out and coming in when he felt like it. She was a good ass girl and everything that Zikhya was not. Tate didn't understand why Mo-T didn't just fuck that bitch and leave her the fuck alone. It was like he was trying to make the hoe into a housewife, and if that was the case he was hustling backwards in the game. Tate heard music blasting from Mo-T's house as he pulled up in the driveway. He was about to set these stupid bitches straight once and for all.

Sequoia felt like her heart stopped after Menijah delivered the horrible message. It was as if the world stood still for a moment. Sequoia just knew she had mistaken what Menijah said. It couldn't be; it just couldn't. She dropped the phone and began to cry from the pit of her soul. The sudden outburst woke Torez out of his sleep. He woke up to find Sequoia in a corner crying uncontrollably, as she held herself and rocked back and forth. He jumped and, ran over to her, and hugged her tight. He didn't ask her any questions because he felt like she would talk when she got ready. After what seemed like an eternity, she finally spoke. " I gave him nine years of my life. I swear before you, I never cheated on my husband Torez, I swear!" cried Sequoia. "I could tell from the first night we spent together. Your body language showed nervousness, Sequoia I know a good woman when I see one" said Torez. "It showed?" asked Sequoia looking up at him through teary eyes and a snotty nose. " Of course it did, you're a rookie" smiled Torez. Sequoia laughed and it felt so good. Suddenly, she pulled Torez towards her and tongue kissed him long, hard, and passionately. Then she stood up and began to rub all over her self starting from her breast down to her clique. Torez had to admit; he was shocked and turned on all at the same time. Sequoia wasn't this open in the beginning and it was no doubt that Torez loved the freaky side that she kept a secret, but he also knew that she was doing everything out of being hurt by her husband. Although he only knew Sequoia for a couple of days, he had cared a great deal about her. She was a good woman and Torez planned to respect her as such. Torez was a man, so if it was any other loose female, he couldn't lie and say that he wouldn't take advantage of a beautiful woman in her time of vulnerability. Sequoia was so much more than that, and he was going to treat her that way. Sequoia proceeded to mount Torez and let all of her frustrations out by riding him like a stallion. Torez was very tempted as he looked at her small firm breast shine in the moonlight as her nipples poked out like small rocks, but he stopped her. Sequoia was puzzled as she looked down at Torez and frowned. " This is the perfect time to get me the way you've always wanted me. Come on Torez, I'm ready" said Sequoia still trying to sit on him. " No, said Torez getting up off the floor and walking away. " No! Oh so now I not only loose my husband, but since you done got the pussy you done with me now too, huh?" asked Sequoia angrily. Torez just looked at her shocked to see her angry side, but he understood. "Now you just going stand there with your arms folded and look at me like I'm fuckin crazy?Okay, you know what, I'm going get my shit and get the fuck out of here. I swear, I'm so tired of niggas. I think Im going get me a fuckin girlfriend!" yelled Sequoia as she packed her things and got dressed wildly, tossing things around. "That wouldn't be a bad idea" smiled Torez fucking with her. He actually thought seeing her mad was cute. " Oh so now you tryna be fucking funny? Now you a comedian, huh? See, that's what the fuck I be talking about with niggas. When Sqeuoia reached the door, Torez grabbed her by the arm and turned her around. " baby listen, you have it all wrong. I understand because of your emotions right now, but if you can't understand that I'm not like most men and I'm not going to take advantage of you at your weak moment. I care for you too much and I just can't do that. " What makes me so special Torez, you don't even know me.

" said Sequoia. "I know enough, I know that you are a very respectable woman. So I want to treat you as such and that's how you should always be treated. You don't know what you're worth because you have been settling for less. Sequoia you deserve to have the whole world in the palm of your hands and you don't even know that. Sequoia started crying all over again. Torez held her face in his hands. "Look at me. I want you to go home and take care of whatever you have to, but don't do anything stupid and take care of yourself. After you get yourself together and you aren't acting off of your emotions and thinking with a clear head, then you contact me. I'll be waiting on you, okay baby?" said Torez kissing Sequoia softly on her lips. She closed her eyes as tears ran down her face and at that moment she secretly wished she had met Torez before she met Mo-T. "You hear me?" he asked her. She nodded her head in agreement and turned to go out the door. She headed to the airport and jumped on the first thing smoking back to Baltimore. She had some business to take care of, so she had to pull it together. When she got back to Baltimore, she planned to raise hell.

"Damn who the fuck banging on the door like that?" asked Zikhya as she started walking over to the window to see if she saw Sequoia's car. "Hold up, sit the fuck down. Let me handle this" Mo-T whispered to Zikhya as he held his gun in position. He had to be on point because it could have been anybody at the rate he was going. He had fucked many females who had husbands and boyfriends and he knew that one day it would come back to haunt him. He hoped that today was not his day, but if it was, fuck it, he wasn't scared to die. "Yo!" yelled Mo-T yelled through the door. "Man open the fuckin door yo!" yelled Tate. Mo-T frowned at how buck Tate was getting with him. Tate knew fuckin' better and when he opened the door, Tate better have a good fuckin reason for coming at him sideways or he was goin get popped, straight like that. " " You some fuckin beef wit me or something nigga?" Mo-T asked Tate. " Man, move your ass out the way, where the fuck that bitch at?" asked Tate asked Mo-T. Just then Zikhya came out of the kitchen dancing to Gucci as she finished up rolling a blunt. " Oh wassup Tate, why the fuck you knocking like you the police nigga" asked Zikhya smiling. Without saying a word tate walked over to Zikya and slapped her so hard, the blunt flew out of her hand and opened back up as the weed flew all over the floor. "YO, WHAT THE FUCK IS YOU DOING SON!" yelled Mo-T as he ran over to Tate and pushed him. Zikhya sat on the floor and held her bleeding lip shoicked by Tate's outburst. " What the fuck is that noise?" asked Raleigh coming out of the basement. POW! The impact from his slap knocked Raleigh back down the basement stairs. "Yo how the fuck you going just come in my house and start slapping bitches yo! What the fuck is you doing man!" yelled Mo-T as he pushed Tate against the wall underneath the staircase as they stood in the living room. "yo, keep your fuckin hands off of me and them bitches know they banked my fuckin baby mother. Weak ass bitches had to bank a pregnant female. "No we didn't bank her. I tried to hold her back from stabbing Zikhya!" yelled Raleigh sitting in th corner next to Zikhya. "Bitch lie in my face again and your ass going back down them fuckin steps! My baby mother not just goin lie and say ya'll banked her if ya'll didn't bitch! She from New York and I know she can take Zikhya and whip your ass with her. My bitch can fight, and when she drop my seed im bringing her to ya'll bitches to fight her one on one. " said Tate. Raleigh and Zikhya were quiet as they rolled their eyes at Tate. "Hold the fuck up, ya'll banked his pregnant baby mother?" asked Mo-T. "Mo-T it wasn't like…. " Zikhya wasn't able to finish. "Bitch shut thefuck up while I'm talking! Ya'll bichtes got a nerve to pull a whore move like that and ya'll suppose to be so fuckin bad?" asked Mo-T. "Ya'll lucky my seed wasn't harmed or I would have killed ya'll bitches!" yelled Tate pointing his finger at Raleigh and Zikhya. "Mo-T I swear we didn't bank her!" yelled Zikhya. "Well what the fuck happened, Zikhya! How the fuck is your story going to be any different from Tate's or Coa-Coa's without being a fucking lie!" yelled Mo-T. "She had a fucking knife! What the fuck was I suppose to do Mo-T?" asked Zikhya. "BITCH, SHE'S PREGNANT DUMB ASS!Of course she's going to protect her and her fuckin seed. She should have cut your stinkin ass. All the fuck you had to do was get in your fuckin car and wait until she had the baby to knuckle up with her and it would have been over. " said Mo-T. " Mo-T I didn't even want to beef with that girl!" lied Zikhya. "Oh you didn't. Well et me ask you this then bitch, why the fuck did you tell her that you fucked Tate then?" asked Mo-T. Zikhya was quiet and that told Mo-T everything he needed to know. "Exactly! Where that other bitch at so I can slap her too!" yelled Tate. " Naw yo, shorty cool. I know she didn't have nothing to do with that shit. She was trying to break it up. " said Mo-T. "How you know Menijah didn't help bank her. She was there too!" yelled Zikhya. " Bitch first of all, don't fuckin question me because Tate's slap is nothing compared to what I'll give you first of all!" yelled Mo-T with veins popping out of his head. Sequoia had shared that look with Zikhya and Raleigh so they knew to shut straight the fuck up. "Mmmmm, ya'll two evil motha fuckas", Raleigh mumbled under her breath. " Bitch if you don't want to take another trip down them steps, I suggest you shut your corn muffin head ass the fuck up while grown men talking!" yelled Tate. Raleigh looked down at the floor while Zikhya didn't dare say one word. " Now, since ya'll want to bank people, ya'll punished. Tate, what do you suggest their punishment be?" asked Mo-T rubbing his chin. "You know what, it will be easy for you to torture Zikhya because she think you her man and she jealous anyway. So I have something in mind for her. Let me think on Raleigh" said Tate rubbing his chin as well. "Alright partner. Well, call baby mother and tell her we taking care of the situation and you spending the day with me to punish these bitches for what they did to her. Oh and tell her, she getting a fair rematch so don't worry" said Mo-T. " That's wassup. My bad about the dumb shit yo, but them bitches could have killed my seed man. She lost so many of my kids yo and now that she finally is able to carry one, you know a nigga pumped the fuck up!" smiled Tate giving Mo-T dap. " I feel you. These bitches doing the dumb shit, stupid ass bitches!" yelled Mo-T. After Tate finished up his phone call with Coa-Coa and everything was cool, him and Tate decided to hit the block. " Check this out. We hittin' the block and we be back. Don't open my fucking door for no fucking body. "said Mo-T. "Yeah and don't answer the phones either!" yelled Tate. " If ya'll try some dumb shit, that's ya'll ass" said Mo-T walking out the door. " That's your ass Mr. Postman" laughed Tate as he walked out the door behind Mo-T. After they heard Mo-T lock the door, they jumped on the phone and called Menijah.

Chapter Seven

"Bitch ya'll lying!" yelled Sequoia. " No we not bitch. He slapped the shit out of us" said Zikhya as she scraped up the weed off the floor and tried to roll it in a fresh blunt. "Menijah he slapped Zikhya so hard, the blunt opened back up and now she scraping the weed off the floor" laughed Raleigh. Menijkah was on the other end of the phone falling out. " Bitch at least he didn't slap me back down the basement steps after I just walked up them motha fuckas" said Zikhya getting an attitude. "Oh shit!" laughed Mainijah. "Bitch why you always catching fucking attitude? Shit, we both got slapped!" yelled Raleigh. "Well bitch stop trying to clown me then! Spark that up. " said Zikhya passing the blunt to Raleigh. "So whatthe fuck ya'll going do while they gone?" asked Menijah "We just have to chill out until they get back" said Raleigh passing the blunt back to Zikhya. "When they coming back?" asked Menijah. "Damn, bitch what the fuck is this, twenty-one questions! Hang up on that hoe!" yelled Zikhya trying to take the cordless phone from Raleigh to hang up in Menijah's ear. "No Zikhya don't be rude!" yelled Raleigh holding the phone away from her. " Alright here, take the blunt and let me talk to her" said Zikhya passing the blunt to Raleigh. "No, Zikhya because I know you are going to hang up on her" said Raleigh. "Bitch, no the fuck I'm not! Now give me the fucking phone!" yelled Zikhya. "Raleigh, don't give her the phone because you kn……". Click! Zikhya up in Menijah's ear. "Zikhya why the fuck did you do that? You a rude ass bitch!" yelled Raleigh. "Bitch so the fuck what! What the fuck can she do to help us, huh? All the fuck she doing is being fuckin nosy so she can probably go back and tell Sequoia" said Zikhya. " I know one thing, she told Sequoia that we all fucked Mo-T" said Raleigh. "I don't give a fuck! I'm ready for whatever, it is what ever the fuck it is forreal. " Said Zikhya. "Yeah, that's what I say" said Raleigh. "She the dumbest bitch I ever knew win my life. Can't even keep a fucking secret because she want to bite Sequoia's ass so brad, bitch!" said Zikhya. "Yeah, she is wild man, but you saw he crying in the room, she not even prepared for the game she trying to be in by hanging with bitches like us" said Raleigh passing Zikhya the blunt. "That bitch don't even have no fight in her" said Raleigh. "Truuuuuue!" yelled Zikhya putting the blunt out in the ashtray that sat on the coffee table. "Now what the fuck are we going to do?" asked Raleigh. " Let's get on the chat line" said Zikhya dialing the number. " Bitch is you crazy! You want another slap don't you?" asked Raleigh. "Bitch I'm not giving them the right name or address. I just want to see howmany dumb mothafuckas come out" said Zikhya. "Alright well go ahead and leave the greeting" said Raleigh, They stayed on the chat line careful to listen out for Mo-T pulling up in the driveway.

"What the fuck is the hold up!" yelled Sequoia at the flight attendant. Mam, please stay calm. We're having technical problems that are out of our control right now. " "Well I have an emergency to get home to, shit!" yelled Sequoia as everybody on the plane looked over in her direction. "What the fuck are ya'll looking at!" she yelled as everybody turned their head away from her. "Mam, you're going to have to keep it down or I'll have no choice but to escort you off of the plane" said the flight attendant. "I'm cool. My bad, look just try to get this problem fixed as soon as possible and bring me a Pepsi" said Sequoia. " No problem Mam, I'll be right back" said the flight attendant. As the flight attendant walked off, she decided to call Menijah since she was calmed down ;at least for the moment. "Hello?" "Hey Ni-Boogie" said Sequoia calling Menijah by the pet name she gave her. "Nothing girl, sitting here polishing my toe nails" said Menijah. "Bitch I know you polishing them black!" laughed Sequoia. "You know it!" laughed Menijah. "So what you been doing all day besides painting them funky ass toes?" asked Sequoia. "Nothing girl, waiting for my Baby Phat dress to come that I ordered off the internet" said Menijah. "Oh shit! Bitch where did you get money from?" "Hooker don't even woory about all that. Just know your girl going be looking fly!" said Menijah. "What occasion did you but it for?" asked Sequoia. "Well you know I told you my cousin Kendra is supposed to be getting married again for the fourth time" said Menijah. "What! Kendra need to stop!" laughed Sequoia. Just then, her other line beeped. "Hold on Menijah, let me see who this is" said Sequoia taking the phone from her ear and looking at the caller ID screen. She saw Mo-T's name flashing and pushed the IGNORE button. "I'm good girl. I'm not clicking over for Mo-T's sorry ass" said Sequoia. "Oh that was him?" asked Menijah feeling butterflies in her stomach at the thought of his name. "Yeah that was his sorry ass" said Sequoia as she took her Pepsi from the flight attendant. The intercom announcement came on that the flight was continuing in routre and that all passengers had to turn off their cell phones. "You hear this bullshit" asked Sequioa. "Yeah, but go ahead and do what you have to do boo. Call me when you touch down" said Menijah. "Alright Ni-Boogie. Thank you for being such a good friend to me for all these years. I don't know what I would do right now without the support of you and Torez. I' am so glad to have a best friend like you" said Sequoia near tears with a tremble in her voice. "Sequoia, I have to ..... . " "Shit! My phone went dead. I'll call her back when I get home" said Sequoia placing her Blackberry in her Gucci purse. She laid back and relaxed as much as she could as she prepared herself to face the music when she hit home.

"Yo, this the last sale and then we shooting up Club Luzerne" Mo-T yelled at Tate as he walked to the corner of Monument and Patterson Park avenue to do a transaction. When they was at the red light, Tate came up with an idea. "Yo, I know what we can do to get them bitches now" said Tate. "Whassup?" asked Mo-T. "Let's turn around and hit Pulaski Highway to go to the Hilton out White Marsh and on our way, let's top at Kings liquor to get some champagne. I can call my homeboy Rosco and get two E-Pills from out Middleriver so everything is in route. " said Tate. "Okay, that's wassup" said Mo-T. After they handled everything, they called Zikhya and Raleigh. Hello?" said Zikhya as she pretended to be sleep. "Get ready. We on our way to drop something off. Go to the Hilton hotel in White marsh and call us when ya'll get there" said Mo-T hanging up without giving Zikhya a chance to respond. " She had the house phone outside leaning in the care talking to the cab driver that took them home from the Lil Wayne concert. She couldn't believe she had ran back into him, but was glad. She had a back up plan just in case things didn't work out with Mo-T. " Alright, well it seem like that call distracted you so you go and handle what you have to handle" said the cab driver Zikhya now knew as Desmond. She was standing outside with a pair of white tight Polo sweat pants with no panties on and a white tee with no bra showing her hard nipples. Not knowing how far away Mo-T was, she wrapped things up with Desmond and ran in the house almost falling on her face from the slippery flip flops. When Mo-T pulled up, they were ready to go and they looked gorgeous. Raleigh had on some faded jean Tye-dye stretch skinny pants that looked painted on. They hugged her ass and showed her phat ass pussy print when she walked. She wore white Roca Wear stilettos and a white halter American Eagle blouse. Zikhya stepped out in red limited edition Sergio three quarter length blouse, a khaki skirt that stopped at her ankles with a split going up between her legs, and red Marc Jacob slip-in high heels. " We have to go to the Hilton hotel in White marsh and call Mo-T and Tate when we get there" said Zikhya. "Well how are we going to get there because your car is at home. " said Raleigh. "I got this, let me make a phone call" said Zikhya. "Hello?" . "Hey babe. Look I'm going to need you for a favor sooner than I thought. " said Zikhya. "How soon?" asked Desmond. "Right now. " said zikhya. "I'm glad I stopped at thisMcDonald right here on Coldspring and Harford before I got too far. I'm on my way back then. " said Desmond. "Okay babe, I 'll see you when you get here", said Zikhya. "Who isthat?" asked Raleigh. "See bitch if your ass wasn't so busy sleeping, you would know I ran back into the cab driver that brought us home after the Lil Wayne concert" said Zikhya. "What! The one who leather you was cracking on?" laughed Sequoia. "Yeah. He coming to pick us up" . Five minutes later, they heard a horn and it was Mo-T and Nate. Zikhya walked up to the truck and took the hotel key. "Don't forget to call us when ya'll first get there. We bought ya'll wine, weed, and got ya'll two E-pills a piece. Take the pills first though. "Why?" asked Zikhya. " Just do it" said Tate as he and Mo-T pulled off. Ten minutes later Desmond pulled up and they got in. " So where we headed to?" asked Desmond. "The Hilton in White Marsh" said Zikhya. Desmond looked back and forth from Zikhya to Raleigh. " Naw, It's not like that. She helping me put something together for my brother, if you know what I mean" said Raleigh. "Oh aight. Well when ya'll think ya'll can come back for pleasure an dnot business?" asked Desmond. "I'll get back toyou on that babe" said Zikhya. The ride took about twenty minutes and that's only because Desmond was driving so damn slow. If Zikhya didn't know any better, she would have sworn he was driving that slow on purpose to savior the moment with her in the car. " Thank you so much" said Zikhya giving Desmond a hug. "No problem, call me agin if you need me" said Desmond driving off. "Alright, the room number is two-thirteen, come on" said Zikhya. When the reached the room, they were elated. Tate and Mo-T had went all out for them. The champagne sat in a bowl with ice and a ribbon was tied on all of the bottles. They were so fixated on the weed, drink, and ecstacy pills that they over looked the note. " Let's get it popping!" yelled Raleigh grabbing the champagne. Go ahead, I'm calling Mo-T to tell him that we here" said Zikhya smoking a blunt.

They was showed much love when they walked into Luzerne's especially by the bitches. "Mo-T, what's up baby? Where the fuck you been at?" asked Tiffany. She was a hoe Mo-T used to fuck with real heavy until she wrote a letter and mailed it to Sequoia telling her everything that was going on between them;the dumb shit! When Mo-T finally caught up with her, he choked the shit out of her ass and left her stranded on the beltway with no way to get home. She damn sure didn't have any money because she got her money through fucking him. Tiffany had some big ass tities, but her ass wasn't all that big. Mo-T didn't give a fuck, she sucked a mean dick. One time she sucked Mo-T and Tae's dick at the same time in the around the corner from Edison Lounge. Tiffany was a fly bitch and she kept herself up. Mo-T and Tate had to give her that. She had chinky eyes and a pretty ass smile. Mo-T loved when she sucked his dick and looked him directly in his eyes as she moaned. That shit always made him cum faster than he intended to. It was all good though, a favor for a favor. "Not too much, what's good with you" asked Mo-T as they hugged and he felt her big ass tities rub up against his chest and her nipples were hard. "This bitch a straight freak" thought Mo-T as he released her. "You know what's up with me, I'm trying to make that money" said Tiffany licking her lips looking down at Mo-T's dick. "That's wassup. I'll holla at you before I bounce", said Mo-T making his way through the crowd. "Hey Tate" said Tiffany hugging him. "What's goin on baby?" TaTe asked Tiffany as he hugged her. He was a big fan of tities and Tiffany's was big just like he liked them "You know what's up with me. Ask Mo-T. " "That's waasup, I'll holla at you though" said Tate right behind Mo-T. "Oh shit! Wassup my niggas! Yelled Mo-T. He hadn't seen Scar, Reggie, Ailee, mike, and Black for a while since the police shut down Rose Street. " Damn it's been a minute!" yelled Reggie as he they all gave each other dap and much love. "This must be my lucky night because I got a proposition for ya'll" said Mo-T. "Wassup?, asked Scar, the head of the crew. "Aight, check this out. We got these two freaks that will do whatever ya'll want and because it's us, they not even worried about getting paid, you follow me?" asked Mo-T. "I'm with you, keep going" said Scar. " Aight now, we already dropped one key off to them and they should be on the way to the hotel now and I told them to call me when they get there. Hold on. Yeah. Thats wassup. Aight so they there, now here go ya'll key. Go talk to take to see how he want shit done because he handle all that. I just set it up", said Mo-T "Aight my nigga, good looking out" said Scar giving Mo-T dap. "It's nothing my nig" said Mo-T going to talk Tiffany "Aight what's the deal?" Scar asked Tae once he reached him at the jukebox. "Okay. Basically these bitches banked my pregnant baby mother over some dumb shit. So I want them to see how it feel to get banked. Mo-T told them to take the pills first, so their dumb ass probably didn't even see the note. Even if they did at this point they too fucked up to understand it anyway. They shared a laugh. Anyway, don't take it easy on them bitches. When ya'll go in there get to business. If they ask where we at, say we not coming and we sent ya'll. Slut them bitches completely out yo, no cut cards. Them bitches could have killed my seed man. I want them dealt with" said Tate. "That's what it is then" said Scar giving Tate dap and waving for his boys to get ready to roll with him. They were on their way to teach Zikhya and Raleigh a lesson that they weren't even ready for. Meanwhile, Tiffany escorted Mo-T and Tate to her house on Glover Street to give them the fuck and suck of their life. Since she missed them, she called four of her home girls over to be of assistance to her Mo-T and Tate were in for something that they would never forget. Tiffany was determined to show Mo-T that nobody can do it like her, not even his wife.

"Yeah Menijah. I just touched own in Baltimore baby. " said Sequoia walking to find her car. "Okay baby. Call me and let me know how everything go" said Menijah. "Will do, love you Ni-Boogie" said Sequoia. "Love you too Quoia-Boo" sid Menijah hanging up. Shit was about to hit the fan real soon and menijah didn't want to be around when it did. " Kendra, what you doing?" asked Menijah. "Girl, nothing getting ready for bed because I have to get up early tomorrow morning . I have an early appointment to go get fitted for my wedding dress, why?" asked Kendra knowing Menijah wanted something. "Come and pick me up", said Menijah. "Well how long are u staying Ni-Boogie because I'm not coming to pick you up if you just going right back home" said Kendra. "Naw. I'm staying for a couple of days" said Menijah. "Oh lord, what your scared ass done did now?" asked Kendra. "Nothing bitch, just come ang get me damn. It don't matter what I do anyway, im your cousin bitch" said Menijah agitated with Kendra. "Whatever, I'm on my way" said Kendra. Menijah packed a few outfits and waited downstairs for Kendra. Fifteen minutes later, she heard a horn beep, it was Kendra. "Come help me with my bags!" yelled Menijah. "Bitch who the fuck you think I'am? Damn, I have to give you a ride and help you with your bags? I'm not fucking you! I think you need to get a man" said Kendra. "Your mutt ass always got something to say" said Menijah. "Bitch I'm not anymore mutt than you since you are my cousin, or did you forget" said Kendra putting the last bagt in the trunk of her black tinted out, year two thousand Impala.

Chapter Eight

Bitch, I cant believe they did this for us" said Raleigh. "I know" said Zikhya. They were feeling woozy off of the pills, but it hadn't taken the full affect on them yet. They were so busy blasting Trina through the speakers that they didn't hear Scar unlock the door . "Ladies, ladies, ladies. Hello to all, might I join this party?asked Scar shutting the door as if he was alone. "Hell yeah as fine as you are" said Raleigh slurring her words. They drowned the four bottles of champagne and had already started on the Henensy XO. "You never lied. Where Mo-T?" asked Zikhya. " Oh he not coming, but I do have some company with me. Would you mind if they join us? asked Scar, "Hell naw! The more the merrier" said Zikhya. Scar opened the door and in came Reggie, Black, Ailee, and Mike. "Damn! The whole crew is fine!" laughed Raleigh barely able to stand up. "Hold up let me call my man to make sure this is okay with him. Mo-T say it's okay, but then he'll get jealous. "Don't even waste your time, ma" laughed Ailee. That was the crew's cue to start taking off their clothes. Raleigh and Zikhya looked on in disbelief as all five of the niggas stripped down to their boxers. They formed a circle around Raleigh and Zikhya so they didn't have no where to run. " Oh ya'll must have over looked the note" said Scar. "What note?" asked Zikhya nervously. "The one folded underneath the wine bowl" said Black. Nervously, Zikhya unfolded the note and almost shitted on herself. It read:

Surprise!!!! Surprise!!!!! Surprise!!!!

Raleigh and Zikhya before ya'll read this, I think ya'll better get comfortable because it's going to be a long night. I'm sure ya'll met my home boys Scar, Reggie, Ailee, Black, and Mike. They going keep ya'll real busy because they heard ya'll got down with banking. That was music to their ears. Hope ya'll like it rough and raw. Don't even think about getting no condoms because they won't use them. These niggas don't give a fuck if they live or die, but they once shared with me that when they did die they wanted to go out fuckin'...LOL.

47

Ya'll bitches going get fucked just like ya'll fucked my baby mother, raw wit no grease. Pay back is a motha fucka dumb bitches!

Your Worst Nightmare,

Tate

P. S. Zikhya don't think about calling Mo-T. He's getting the fuck of his life by four sexy ass bitches. You are the farthest thing from his mind.

"Raleigh, they set us up" said Zikhya. "That's right bitches so assume the fucking position, panties off, ass up" said Scar rubbing his hands together. The train they ran on Zikhya and Raleigh is something the girls wouldn't wish on their worst enemy. Scar grabbed Raleigh and slammed her asshole down on his dick. "Aaaahhhhhh!", yelled Raeigh. Ailee came in front of her and rammed his dick down her throat. She gagged and began to vomit, but Ailee didn't care. "If you take my dick out your mouth bitch, I swear I'm going shoot your ass!" said Ailee holding the gun to her temple. Raleigh had no choice but to keep going, vomit and all. Mike grabbed Zikhya by her hair, and slung her on the bed. "Open your mouth bitch!" Reggie yelled at Zikhya. Zikhya did as she was told and felt warm urine filling up her mouth. "Just like a nut" laughed Mike and Black. Black, Reggie, and Mike all shoved their dick in Zikhya mouth at once. She felt like her mouth was ripping apart. Black pulled out and put Zikhya's legs behind her head as he rammed his dick in her. He fucked her rough and hard. His dick was so deep in her, he felt his balls slapping up against her thighs. "Pleeeease stop!" yelled Zikhya, but it was no use. Reggie and Black slapped their dicks on Zikhya's face until cum covered her entire face. Then all five of them grabbed Raleigh and sexually violated her over and over until lay numb. When they let her loose, her body was covered in urine, vomit, and cum. She smelled horrible but she didn't care, all she could do was lay in a fetal position shaking. She had never felt so violated in her life. She made up her mind while laying in semen amd urine that she was done living her life like she was. She promised herself that from that day forward she would live her life straight. The five friends did the same to Zikhya, but she tried to put up a fight. That was the wrong thing to do, the guys beat her to no end while Raleigh lay on the bed in a state of shock shaking. "Come on yo, let's get the fuck out of here before one of the neighbors call them boys!", yelled Scar as they all rushed to get dressed. "Don't you ever in your life swing on a nigga like me! I could have killed your dumb ass bitch!" yelled Ailee as he back hand slapped Zikhya. "Yeah bitch you try that shit with Mo-T and Tate but you don't fuck with the Rose Street boys hoe!" yelled Mike. "We from a different breed bitch and we will end your life and feel nothing!" yelled Reggie. "Please, just leave, Pleeeeeease!" cried Zikhya blocking herself with her arms. "I think our lesson stuck, let's be out" said Scar as the sound of police sirens in the distance caught their attention. "You alright Raleigh?" asked Zikhya. "Yeah, I can't believe Mo-T and Tate would do something like this to us" said Raleigh. " Well bitch, believe it" said Zikhya. "I got some niggas that will kill all them mothafuckas, remember them niggas we met down south when we went to Myrtle Beach?" asked Raleigh. "Yeah I remember. Raleigh, maybe what just happened to us is karma from all the dirt we've done. Playing tic for tat with them crazy motha fuckas is only going to make things worse. I mean come on, them niggas live down south. What if they come here to Baltimore, handle Mo-T and them for us, and they find out we were behind it when them niggas go back home?" asked Zikhya. "Oh my goodness, Zikhya are you feeling okay? I know this is not the Zikhya who is out to get what she want and could care less about the consequences" added Raleigh sarcastically. "Raleigh, them niggas could have killed us!" yelled Zikhya. "I know, but they didn't. I don't care what you say, them niggas is just not coming in this hotel room, violating me and have no consequences for it. "if you waqnt to let it go like that, then go ahead. I know damn well I'm not!" yelled Raleigh. "okay Raleigh do whatever you're going to do. Just promise me two things?" asked Zikhya. "What's that?" asked Raleigh. "Promise me that you'll let things die down first and that you'll be extra careful" said Zikhya. "I promise I'll be careful, but them motha fuckas are going to pay for what they did to us" said Raleigh. "Okay, give me a hug" said Zikhya. The girls hugged eachother as they both cried. Zikhya was mad at herself that she introduced Raleigh into the raw life of the streets. Raleigh was a good wholesome girl who went to church every day of the week before Zikhya turned her out. "Every man out here for self, so always play the game like you hungry. Never take shorts or let a motha fucka bitch you. It's always a motha fucka out there who's going to test you, but when they do you go after them with the deadliest revenge you can seek out. " Zikhya remembered telling Raleigh. Now she was regretting it because her mentality now ran through Raleigh's blood and she knew there was no changing her back. Zikhya decided not to waste her time trying to solve a useless case and concentrated on where she would move to change her life around. Being a click away from death was the only wake up call she needed. She felt for Raleigh, but she had to look out for herself. When shit popped off, she damn sure wasn't going to be anywhere around. Before she left, she made a promise to face Sequoia and tell her the truth.

Sequoia saw the living room lights on when she finally pulled up in front of her house. Surprisingly, Mo-T had cut the grass and the lawn looked neat. "How the hell did he find time to do that with all that hoeing he do? He probably paid somebody to do it with his lazy ass" thought Sequoia. She walked up the steps and turned her key in the door to find Mo-T, Tate, and Nook bagging up weed at the kitchen table. They had the music blasting Tupac and there were soda cans, food wrappings, and blunt paper every where. "Wassup baby! When did you get back?" "Wassup baby my motha fuckin ass! Nook and Tate ya'll need to get the fuck out because I got some shit to handle with my husband!" yelled Sequoia snatching her Vera Wang shades off of her face. "No problem. How was your trip ma?" asked Tate as him and Nook gathered their pack and headed to the door. "Tate, not right now, I'll talk to you when I calm down" said Sequoia giving him the most evilest look she could. "My bad" said Tate throwing his hand up in the air. "Can I get a hug?" asked Nook. "Nook don't keep fucking playing with me!" yelled Sequoia as she picked up a hammer. Nook and Tate ran out the front door laughing. "That nigga in for some shit" . "Hell yeah yo, I bet it got something to do with that hoe Zikhya" Sequoia heard Tate and Nook say on their way to their car. "So everybody know huh?" asked Sequoia pacing back and forth in the kitchen. "Sequoia, I'm so…. . " "You know what Mo-T, don't even fucking say it! You know why, because you not fucking sorry. Out of all the sluts in this fucking world, you had to not sleep with one of my best friends, but two!" yelled Sequoia. "Baby, I tried to tell you them bitches wasn't shit and now you see" said Mo-T. Sequoia had to laugh to keep from stabbing his ass. "Okay, so let me get this straight. You fucked two out of the three of my best friends because you wanted to teach me a lesson. You know what, you are a dirty dick, soon to have AIDS, walking fucking disease Mo-T!" yelled Sequoia. Mo-T just kept his head down the entire time she yelled because he knew he was wrong. He noticed she was leaving Menijah out of the situation which meant she was the snitch. She was smart enough to leave herself out though, but if that made Sequoia feel even a little bit better that she thought she had someone in her corner than he would leave it alone. After all, Sequoia was the one in pain right now and he didn't want to cause her anymore. "So now you don't have anything to say? You just gong continue to soit there and look stupid, SAY SOMETHING MOTHA FUCKA YOU OWE ME A DAMN EXPLANATION!!!" Sequoia yelled in his face. "Sequoia, I don't feel anything for them bitches. I just did it to get you away from them before they sucked you into the trifling life they in" said Mo-T. "You a fuckin trip. How are you going to call my friends sluts, freaks, and trash but you turn right around and fuck and suck them? Don't say you didn't eat their pussy because I know how your nasty ass get down!" said Sequoia. "Not both of them!" yelled Mo-T. "Mo-T it don't fuckin matter, it was trifling! Now you got a favorite, huh? Well who was the special back stabbing bitch that got her pussy ate by my husband?" asked Sequoia with her hands on her hips looking at Mo-T? Mo-T rubbed his head and cursed at his self. "Don't regret it now because you wasn't regretting it when you was doing it! NOW WHICH ONE WAS IT!" yelled Sequoia grabbing a knife. "Zikhya" mumbled Mo-T. "You dumb motha fucka, you was better off doing Raleigh! Now you done put your mouth on the whole city of Baltimore! Stupid motha fucka!" yelled Sequoia. There was silence as Sequoia gathered her thoughts. "***Look at me. I want you to go home and take care of whatever you have to, but don't do anything stupid and take care of yourself***" Sequoia remembered Torez saying. Suddenly, she calmed down realizing she wasn't completely innocent either. She had some explaining to do as well, but right now she was running the show. "So tell me one more thing, did you use protection?" Sequoia asked with her back toward Mo-T. She waited for an answer and when she didn't get one, she knew what it was. She fell to her knees and cried like she never cried before. To know what she felt, a woman would have experienced what she did. It was like a pain that able to be cured. She felt embaressed, betrayed, alone, and like a failure. "What did I do wrong Mo-T, just tell me please!" Sequoia cried holding on to Mo-T as tight as she could. "MAN, FUCK!" yelled Mo-T kicking one of the expensive plants in their living room across the floor and watched as it hill the wall busting open. "I'm sorry baby, I swear I never want to break you down like this Sequoia. " Mo-T cried as he held her in his arms. They both cried until they couldn't cry anymore. When Sequoia gathered herself together, she stood up and wiped her eyes as she walked to the door. "Sequoia, please don't leave me baby. I fucked up and I promise I'll get help. We can go to marriage counseling or anything you want baby, just please don't leave me alone" said Mo-T. Sequoia kept her back turned to him. She wanted to take her husband back so bad, but this time she knew she couldn't. Mo-T had crossed the line and everytime she saw Raleigh or Zikhya it would remind her of the pain. How could she have sex with her husband without thinking about how he had sex with Raleigh and Zikhya. On top of that, the trust was now history. Sequoia knew it was over, but she still needed closure. All of Mo-T's begging fell on death ears and Mo-t needed to face the fact that his begging would not work any longer. "I need to clear my head for a while and I'll be back to get my belongings . On that day I want a meeting with you, Raleigh, and Zikhya. I'm bringing Menijah with me when I come so neither one of them can lie about anything. Before I move on, I need the truth about everything Mo-T. " said Sequoia. "Sequoia, please think about what I said, please" said Mo-T grabbing her hand. Sequoia pulled away and opened the door. "The meeting will be held here at noon, so make sure everyone is on time" said Sequoia as she walked to her car. After the meeting, she could move on with her life completley, maybe with Torez;who knows? After she left, Mo-T practically drank his life away. He knew it was over and that he had fucked up big time. He cried and got drunk all night long. He didn't answer the phone or the door. He stayed in his misery until he passed out to sleep.

Chapter Nine

"Yeah, so ya'll handled ya'll business?" Tate asked Scar one night as they sat in Coa-Coa's benz smoking Purple. "Man them bitches was screaming, aaaahhhh, aaaahhhh, please leave! Them assholes was on fire!" laughed Scar and Tate. "That's what them bitches get" said Tate. "Yeah son, it's all good, appreciate the love. Call me when you get some more hoes that need some hood lessons. BOOM! The back car window burst open and more bullets kept coming. Tate was glad he kept the car running. He quickly put the car in drive and sped off. Go head and drive while I bust my gat out the window!" yelled Scar. Tate was driving as fast as he could, but as much as Scar was shooting, the black SUV was on their ass. "Man you doing all that shooting, hit that motha fucka so they can get off our ass!" yelled Tate getting frustrated. " He tried calling Mo-T several times, but kept getting his answering machine. " Nigga answer the fuckin phone man! These niggas bustin at us yo, pick up the fuckin phone!" yelled Tate hanging up to focus back on driving. "Nigga shut the fuck up and drive!" yelled Scar loading back up. This time he took his time, aimed, and shot directly at the front windshield causing the car to loose control and swerve hitting a curb. "Yo, it's about seven or eight of them motha fuckas!" yelled Scar. Even as they got away, they were still getting shot at. Suddenly, Tate made a u-turn. "Yo what the fuck is you doing!" yelled Scar. "I'm going to see who these motha fuckas is and who sent them!" yelled Tate. "Motha fucka is you crazy! It's about ten of them niggas up against two of us!" yelled Scar. "Nigga well I'll drop your bitch ass off and go by my motha fuckin self cause I'm not about to let no punk ass niggas shoot at me and run from them. I'm going to handle this shit now nigga so is you down or not cause I don't have a lot of time to waste" said Tate. "Nigga you already know what it is" said Scar. "That's what the fuck I'm talking about" said Tate giving Scar dap. "Alright this what we going do. We going park two blocks down from where they start busting at us. Then we going come up behind them niggas and just start busting and we not stopping until all them niggas hit the ground, you got me?" asked Tate. "Got you" said Scar. "Alright nigga then let's do this" said Tate. They parked the car as planned and carried lots of ammo. "They got one of ours and we got one of theirs yo, so fuck it" yelled one of the dudes. "Man where the fuck is the ambulance at!" yelled the other dude. "Right here motha fucka!" yelled Tate bustin everything standing, even innocent by standers. "Oh shit!" yelled the dudes as they started running, but it was no use. Tate and Scar laid them niggas down one by one, sure not to kill them until they got the information they needed. They walked up on one of the dudes while he was breathing heavy holding his chest trying to crawl. Tate put his foot on smashed his foot down on the dude leg where he had been shot. "Awwwww! Fuck you motha fucka! I didn't do it man, it wasn't me!", he yelled. "Well who sent you motha fucka!" yelled Tate aiming his gun at the dude's head. "Nigga suck my dick!" yelled the dude. Tate instantly let off his whole clip in the dude. Scar was pistol whipping two of the other dudes at the same time trying to get answers out of them. "Nigga your life can end right fuckin now, who the fuck sent you nigga!" yelled Scar. "I'm not telling you shit!" yelled the one of the dudes. "Yeah nigga we GA for life motha fucka!" yelled the other dude. Scar put a single bullet through both of their heads. They went through four more dudes and got no answers. When they got to the last one, they knew he was their only hope so they stepped to him with a different approach. "I see ya'll some loyal niggas" said tate standing over top of the dude. He said nothing as he held his arm while blood poured out of it. "Check this out man, I got a seed on the way. It's my first one and I'm trying to be around for shorty and I know you feel that from one man to another" said Tate. The boy still said nothing. Look, we need to know the motha fuckas who sent you and your crew so we can handle them. You know the code of the streets. "I'm still going to die if I tell you though, right?" asked the dude frowning as he continued to hold his arm. Tate was silent as he stared at him in his face. That was all the dude needed to know his answer. "Dig in my pocket" said the dude. Tate looked at Scar and nodded. Scar dug in the dude's pocket first pulling out his wallet. "Yo, let this man go yo, he only sixteen" said Scar. Tate looked at him like he was stupid. "Keep digging" said the dude. Scar finally pulled out a picture of a two beautiful twin spanish little girls. "They my babies, amn. That's Zion on the left and that's Zina on the right. Call the number on the back and give them my love. " said the young boy. After hearing that, Tate couldn't do it, if it was up to him, he wouldn't have. It wasn't up to him, it was up to the code of the streets. Niggas knew that no witness was a dead witness. "Handle that son" said Tate as he walked off toward the car. Tate could do a lot of things, but killing a kid wasn't one. When he heard the single shot, a tear fell down his face as he heard Scar running to catch up with him. " Come on nigga let's get the fuck out of here, I'm driving" said Scar as hopped in the driver seat, waited for Tate to jump in the car and sped off. " Raleigh set it up" said Scar.

"Hell yeah girl, them niggas probably busting at them niggas right now" Raleigh bragged on the phone to Zikhya and Menijah. "Girl your ass better be careful" said Menijah. "That's what I told her" said Zikhya. "Girl, but fuck that. Guess hwo called me sounding all sad and shit?" asked Zikhya. "Who" asked Raleigh and Menijah at the same time. "Mo-T" . "Mo-T! He wasn't with Tate when they got hit up?" asked Raleigh. "See bitch you playing a game that you don't know shit about" said Zikhya. "Girl you should have had all that shit straight before you put the hit out" said Menijah. "Well, it don't matter because that nigga got his coming to him too" said Raleigh. "Anywaaaay, girl he talking about I fucked his life up and him and Sequoia was beefing. Then he going say if it wasn't me he cheated with she wouldn't have left and all this dumb shit" said Zikhya. "I think she would have because she was tired of his shirt anyway" said Menijah. "Yeah, them he going say Sequoia want a meeting with all of us to get closure to move on and that if we didn't come he was going to personally whip all of our ass" said Zikhya. "Where is the meeting going to be held?" asked Menijah. "He said Sequoia want it at the house" said Zikhya. " Oh okay" said Menijah. Just then her line beeped, it was Sequoia. "Alright bitches, well I have to go. My new boo calling me on the other end" lied Menijah. "Oh bitch please, he'll be gone by the end of this week" said Zikhya. "Bitch stop hating!" said Menijah. "Never!" said Zikhya as she heard Menijah click off the three-way. " So you sure nobody followed you to that hotel, right?"asked Zikhya. "Girl, stop being so paranoid, I'm straight" said Raleigh. "Alright girl, I just worry about you. I still think you should have went to a further location soit won't be so easy for them Tate and them to find you just in case one of them niggas you sent did rat you out" said Zikhya. "Awwww, I love you too. Them niggas is too thorough, Tate is no comparison to their army. Girl they southern warriors, you don't know?" asked Raleigh. "Alright girl, well I'm going to bed. Call me if you need me" said Zikhya. "Okay girl, love you" said Raleigh. Love you too" said Zikhya as she hung up. She knew how Tate and his crew got down and knew that Raleigh's life was on the line.

"Hey Sequoia wassup?" asked Menijah. "Nothing girl, just left Mo-T and I need somebody to talk to" said Sequoia sadly. "Awww, well what did he say?" asked Menijah. "I don't even want to talk about it" said Sequoia near tears once again. "Okay, so where are you going to stay?" asked Menijah. "I'm renting out a hotel room for a week. When the week is up, I'm going to get my things from the house and hold a meeting with him, Raleigh, and Zikhya. I know that you had nothing to do with it Menijah, but I need you there for support because you are about the only honest one out of this whole mess, said Sequoia. Menijah wanted to cry out and tell her that she was part of it too, but she just couldn't bring herself to do it. She knew it would crush Sequoia to know that she didn't have not one true friend after all they'd been through together. "Okay, I'll go with you. What time?" "Monday at noon. I'll pick you up and we'll ride together" said Sequoia. "Oh that's okay, I can get Kendra to bring me" said Menijah trying her best to make Sequoia change her mind. "No Menijah, it's okay I can come and pick you up. " "Kendra can bring me because she's going to be driving through that way anyway to pick out the theme of her wedding decorations" said Menijah trying her hardest to get out of riding to the meeting with Sequoia. It was bad enough that she was talking to her on the phone like she had done nothing wrong. She couldn't dare ride in her car to the meeting with her after what she had done. "Menijah, I really need you. I promise not to keep crying, I'll try to keep it together because I know it bothers you to see me upset. It always have " said Sequoia. "Okay, well stay strong and hang in there" said Menijah. "I'll try. Go ahead, I know you have things to do. I just want to thank you again for being my one and only true friend. If it weren't for you, I don't even know if I could be this strong" said Sequoia. "You know you don't have to thank me Sequoia, we're like sisters and I'll always be here for you" said Menijah. "I know, well goodnight" said Sequoia. "Goodnight" said Menijah. Menijah felt more guilty than she ever had in her entire life.

"Baby, what happened!" yelled Coa-Coa running to Tate as soon as he came through the door. It seemed like her belly was growing over night and it was huge. She was going to have the baby a month early because she was dilating too fast. Her and Tate were having sex everyday, several times a day. Tate had heard of pregnancy making some females uncomfortable about having sex. Coa-Coa wasn't one of those females, she loved it and Tate was glad that she did. As a matter of fact, she wanted it more than he did. He figured it must be her New York genes, but whatever it was he didn't care and was always ready to get down. "Baby be careful, stop running" said Tate taking ofyf the hoody that blood splashed on when he shot the first dude. "Baby are you okay!" yelled Coa-Coa feeling all over his body cjecking for bullet holes. "baby, I'm fine. Calm down" said Tate kissing Coa-Coa and rubbing his fingers through her hair. She lkaid her head on his chest abnd listened to his heartbeat. "Baby I don't know what me and the baby would do without you" said Coa-Coa. "Ya'll won't ever have to know what that's like" said Tate kissing the top of her head. "Why do you have all that blood on you if you're okay?" said Coa-Coa. "Don't worry about all that baby, go get some rest" said Tate. "I'm not going to bed without you" said Coa-Coa holding om to him. " Baby go ahead upstairs. I'm coming right behind you, I promise" said Tate. "No Tate, I almost lost you! Do you fuckin understand how I feel right now? I don't want to leave your side ever agin now!" yelled Coa-Coa crying. Tate hgated that she was so emotional sometimes, but he knew it was the pregnancy. "Coa-Coa, listen to me. I really need you to go upstairs baby. Some shit went down and I need a moment alone. I'll be upstairs in ten minutes" said Tate. "Five" said Coa-Coa. "Ten minutes Coa-Coa, go upstairs" said Tate in a firm voice trying his best not to get upset with Coa-Coa. "You always get what you want and I never get what I want" said Coa-Coa pouting as she stomped up the stairs and slammed the bedroom door. Tate thought it was cute before she got pregnant, but he was going to have to break her out of that shit now. She couldn't go around acting like a child when she was about to have one. Tate walked slowly to the kitchen table, sat down, and cried like he never did before. The fact that a sixteen year old had to loose his life all over a code in the street was eating at him. He had no choice because if he didn't do it, then it would be him lying dead on the ground. Tate was interrupted by his cell phone vibrating on his hip. "Talk to me" he said. "Yo I just got your meassage, you straight son!" yelled Mo-T. "Man, we laid all them niggas down. I'm just fucked up in the head right now because one of them little niggas was only sixteen son" said Tate wiping his eyes. As ruthless as he was, he had a heart. "Man, fuck him. Better him than you" said Mo-T. Mo-T was the one with a heart made of steel. He would kill an infant child if he had to and think nothing of it. "Word" said Tate. "I'm ready for some wreck any way nigga. You know Sequoia leaving me, right" asked Mo-T near tears again. Tate heard his sadness through the phone. Out of nowhere, Mo-T broke down and cried. "I can't loose her yo, I can't fucking loose her Tate!" yelled Mo-T as he started banging the phone against the wall. Tate hung up because he hated to see his boy broken like that. He wiped his eyes and went upstairs with his girlfriend and soon to arrive baby boy. Coa-Coa went to the doctor's office early that morning and found out she was having a boy. She couldn't wait to share the good news with Tate because that's what he wanted. "I talked to Sequoia and she is fucked up about that shit yo" said Coa-Coa. "Yeah, Mo-T just called me when I was down stairs and he was on the phone loosing it his self. " said Tate. "Yeah she told me that her, Mo-T, Raleigh, Zikhya, and Menijah was going to having a meeting. She said she needed it to get closure so she could move on with her life. "Oh forreal, when is this going to take place and what time?" asked Tate. "I think she said this coming Sunday at noon. Why Tate because I know you not trying to go to that meeting to see your little fucking girlfriend" said Coa-Coa sitting up in bed looking at Tate. "I'm not going so shut the fuck up and lay down. You don't even know what the fuck you talking about" said Tate agitated with Coa-Coa. That was all Tate needed to know. After Coa-Coa fell asleep, he snuck back downstairs to make a phone call. "Yeah Scar wassup my nig? I got another proposition for you" said tate. "Damn nigga, you got some more pussy lined up already? You a bad man!" laughed Scar. Tate chuckled, Scar was a funny dude. "Naw man, this on some other shit. Check this out. Mo-T and his wife setting up a candy store so they can get some extra money this Monday at one o'clock in the afternoon. Raleigh is going to be there and I want you to keep track of how much candy she buying;she can go over board sometimes. After she buy the candy I want you to make sure she gets home safe because you know how it is in them streets. After she get home, call me so I don't worry. Feel me?" asked Tate. "Loud and clear" said Scar hanging up. He understood the code Tate was speaking and he was more than glad to do the job. Not to mention he was going to get some more of that good pussy before he sent her to her maker. His dick got hard just thinking about it. Raleigh tried once again to Tate from his family and no one seemed to know where she was. She could run but, she couldn't hide and when he caught up with her this time, he would make sure that she would have no more chances to threaten his future with his family ever again.

Chapter Ten

Six months seemed to fly by and before Sequoia knew it, the day for the meeting had arrived. It was a beautiful sunny summer day. Birds were chirping, kids were playing, ice cream trucks were out, hustlers on the corner doin' their thing, and ghetto kids were getting wet by the fire hydrant. She was on her way to pick up Menijah so they could get a bite to eat before the meeting. Menijah seemed to be more nervous about the meeting than Sequoia was and she was acting really strange. "You look cute, where you get that scarf from? I like that girl, I'm going to have to borrow that" said Sequoia. "Girl, Kendra let me hold this, but I think she ordered it off the internet off of the Saks Fifth site, like she do all of her clothes. " said Menijah. "Well that's probably why I never saw it then. What you want to eat?" Sequoia asked Menijah. Menijah was looking out of the window in her own world, she didn't even hear Sequoia ask her a question. "Menijah, Menijah!" yelled Sequoia. "Oh, my bad. You was callin' me?" asked Menijah, embarrassed that Sequoia had caught her staring into space. "Menijah, what is up with you? You have been acting strange veery since I picked you up, is there something bothering you that you want to talk about? You know you my sister and I'll always be here for you to talk to" said Sequoia. "Naw, um, I'm good. I probably just eat from Dairy Queen, I like their hotdogs. " "Alright well I guess I'll eat from there too" said Sequoia pulling up in the drive-thru to order their food. Menijah was a nervous wreck the entire time. She had a gut feeling that the meeting was going to go out of control. If Zikhya was going to be there, she knew that if she had to go down she was taking a lot of people down with her starting with Menijah. Only this time, there wouldn't be anywhere for Menijah to run and she would have no choice but to face Sequoia. "Check that bag to make sure our orders are right" said Sequoia breaking her thoughts. "Yeah, we good" said Menijah eating a French fry. They ate on their way to Sequoia's house and soon they were pulling up in the driveway. They saw Zikhya's car so they knew Raleigh was present as well. She was Zikhya's puppy, she sniffed her ass everywhere she went. If Sequoia didn't know any better, she would have sworn that

59

Raleigh was starting to believe that she actually was Zikhya. She could be wrong, but lately it was just the way Raleigh had been acting. Sequoia heard about the hit she had put out on Mo-T and Tate for setting her and Zikhya up to get rapped. The front desk clerk was Sequoia's father's ex girlfriend Leslie. She recognized Raleigh when she checked into the hotel. When Raleigh was on the phone running her big mouth, Leslie was walking past her room to check the availability for a presidential suite that a customer was requesting. As soon as Leslie got back downstairs, she called Sequoia to let her know. That was what the fuck Mo-T get for fuckin' with some ghetto ass bitches that don't give a fuck about him. She was going to let him handle that shit on his own so he could know how it felt to be betrayed. Tricey Birmingham, Sequoia's mother had hated on Leslie on a regular basis. Sequoia liked Leslie because she was real cool, she didn't care that her father cheated on her mother with her. Leslie took time out to do things with Sequoia that Tricey didn't because she was too busy chasing her next high. She was just happy that her father found happiness, even if it wasn't with her mother. Her father's smile was the only thing that mattered to her. Kenard "PIMPIN HOES" Birmingham was the hood known ladies man, until some clown ass nigga ran up on him and shot him in his head for fucking with his wife. Mo-T reminded her so much of her father with his cheating ways, that's why it was so hard for her to leave him. She watched her father cheat on her mother for years, so she kind of understood that it was a man thing and he was going through a phase. Cheating is one thing, but Mo-T took it to a whole other level and it was no way she could take him back again. This time, she simply couldn't do it and there were a lot of reasons why. She took a deep breath as she prepared to enter the house she once considered her home. "You ready Ni-Boogie?" she asked Menijah. When she looked over at her, she looked as if she had seen a ghost. "Girl if your ass don't stop going into space mode, I'm going throw some cold water on your ass! Come on" laughed Sequoia. Sequoia may have been laughing, but there was nothing funny at all to Menijah because she knew what was about to go down. When they entered the house, everybody was sitting at the family table that seated twelve guest in the kitchen. Her and Zikhya locked eyes as Sequoia stared a hole through her, but Zikhya didn't back down. "Baby, not now. You said a meeting not a fight. " said Mo-T getting up out of his chair to stand in front of Sequoia. Sequoia thought about what Torez said once again, and slowly sat down in her chair. She was above Zikhya and she wasn't going to stoop down to her level. She looked at what

Zikhya had on. As usual, she looked like a stray hooker. Sequoia wore a off white Vera Wang pin stripe business pant suit with diamond cuff links and Gucci heels. It was a limited edition and it was bad! All eyes were on her as she strutted across the living room floor to the kitchen. Menijah never had style because she was in too much of a comfort zone. When they went out, Sequoia or Zikhya would dress her up. She wore an Ed Hardy T-shirt with a pair of Calvin Klein jeans and a pair of air force ones. Zikhya had on a orange, white, and brown sequenced colored, spandex material, Apple Bottom dress with a hood. Sequoia had to admit it was cute, but not something she would wear. Zikhya's stomach was sitting out further than usual, but Sequoia quickly shook that thought out of her mind; it hurt too bad to think about. Even though Mo-T fucked up, she still had her reputation to uphold. Anybody who knew Sequoia knew she always kept her shit tight and she stayed classy, no matter what. Zikhya had on a pair of brown Stacy Adams, snake skin, thigh high "come-fuck-me boots and a real cute Juicy Cotoure clutch to blend with her dress sitting with her legs wide open. If that was what Mo-T wanted to trade her in for, he could have that. The least he could have done was get some competition for her. She had to laugh to herself as she crossed her legs and folded her habds on the table top like a lady. Zikhya rolled her eyes in her head. Raleigh looked pathetic because she was just copying off of Zikhya. That was so not her and Sequoia wished she would just be herself. Raleigh wore a pair of faded jean shorts that were so tight, the zipper wouldn't even stay up. She was laughing all up in Zikhya's face and didn't know how satupid and ridiculous she looked. She thought it was cute and that was the sad part of it all. She wore a G-Unit blouse that was full of lint balls and had a ton of powder on her neck . Sequoia looked at Raleigh and shook her head "Who does that?" she asked herself. "Wassup menijah? I see you got to ride wit' ya girl, that's wassup" laughed Zikhya giving Raleigh a high five. Menijah wanted to disappear through t he floor. She hated when Zikhya was so childish. "Alright, well first of all, I want to say that I am a Christian and I try to go strictly by the bible. I' am here to get closure for myself so that I may move on and have a better life without baggage from this situation. I just want the truth from everybody, starting with you Mo-T. How this all of this come about?" asked Sequoia. "When we talked on the phone when I was at private stock that night, that's when shit got poppin'. I was drunk as a motha fucka and I wasn't thinking, man. "Where did this little escapade take place?" asked Sequoia rubbing her chin. The tension in the air was so thick as silence filled the room. Sequoia knew the answer, and laughed out loud to keep from crying. "Keep going" she told Mo-T. "So, um, like I was saying. I was tryna leave out forreal and shorty started grabbin' on my clothes talkin bout stop playin' games wit her and she wanna fuck me and all that. So…" "Mo-t stop tryna ct like I was all on your dick because you was talkin shit to me too! Talkin about I been watching that big phat red ass all night and I knew it. You a fuckin dog and Sequoia already know it" said Zikhya. "Bitch what the fuck are you, you scandalous ass hoe! You fucked my marriage up bitch!" Mo-T yelled as he stood up, this time Sequoia stood up to block him. "Nigga I wish the fuck you would put your hands on me!" yelled Zikhya tryna show off. "Bitch what thefuck you goin do!" yelled Mo-T with veins poppin' out of his head. "Zikhya, I'm tellin' you what I know. In a minute, I'm not going to be able to hold Mo-T back, so I advice you to sit the fuck down and shut the fuck up. That's exactly what she did. "Anyway baby, like I was saying…" "Baby, oh nigga you so fuckin phoney!" laughed Zikhya. "Yo, I swear to god, if you cut me off one more fuckin time, I'm goin put your head through that fuckin' wall!" yelled Mo-T meaning every word he said and Zikhya knew it. "I mean basically I fucked her and that was it. We never talked about being in a relationship or no shit like that. She been wantin' to fuck me Sequoia since we met on the cruise that year on Menijah's birthday. When everybody was picking out a girl to grab, she feel like I should have picked her. She had a thing for me the whole nine years we been together" said Mo-T. Sequoia sat in her seat showing no expression which she knew everybody was dying to see. She remained strong. "So how do you come into play Raleigh?" asked Sequoia looking down at the table because she couldn't look at Raleigh. Raleigh didn't look a bit interested in the meeting as she looked up from picking her long nails. "Huh? Oh well, I was just with Zikhya one night when me, Mo-T, Nook, and Tate went to a hotel room and had sex with each other" said Raleigh. Mo-T waited for Sequoia's reaction, but got nothing. "Thanks for telling me the truth Zikhya and Raleigh, even though Menijah is the only honest friend in this room. I can't say if I'll forgive ya'll, but right now I'm speaking with my emotions as ya'll can see. I think I've taken all that I could take so I'm going to go pack now. Come with me Menijah" said Sequoia standing up out of her seat. "Honest? How that bitch honest when she fucked him too!" yelled Zikhya. Sequoia stiffened up and stood completely still. It was as if a demonic spirit over took her when she heard those words. Being a Christian soon went out the door as she watched the stupid look on Menijah's face that confirmed Zikhya's truth. She jumped on Menijah and started pounding on her face that she was a dummy doll. BITCH YOU SAID YOU HAD MY BACK! YOU SUPPOSE TO BE MY SISTER! I CRIED TO YOU EVERY NIGHT AND YOU KNEW THE WHOLE TIME! I TOLD YOU MY DEEPEST SECRETS, BITCH I HATE YOU!" screamed Sequoia as she sat on top of Menijah and banged her head on the hard floor. Her head bust open in the back and blood gushed out all over the kitchen floor. "Aaaaaaaarrrrgggh! Somebody get this crazy bitch off of meeee!" yelled Menijah. "Mo-T, Zikhya, and Raleigh looked on in disbelief with their mouths hung open as Sequoia whipped Menijah's ass. Zikhya and Raleigh started walking toward Sequoia but she didn't see them. "Ya'll bitches better back the fuck up! Fuck ya'll think this is, I will blow both of yua'll motha fuckin brains out if ya'll ever think ya'll going bank my wife. I will put a hole through ya'll motha fuckin head and sit wit ya'll bopdies until the police come! Fuck is wrong with ya'll, ya'll don't know who ya'll fuckin wit!" said Mo-T aiming his guns at Zikhya and Raleigh. They backed up as they saw Mo-T's eyes turn a bright blood shot red. "Oh. Ya'll bitches wanna bank me! Well bitches I wanna fight ya'll one on one! Let's get it done!" yelled Sequoia taking off her suit jacket and her high heels. She was ready to throw hammers as she put her guards up like a nigga. Mo-T had created a monster and he knew Zikhya nd Raleigh was about to get their ass whipped hood B-More style. Mo-T taught her everything she knew and it stuck with her. "Bitch you aint sayin nothing!" yelled Zikhya taking off her heels and earrings. "Wassup them bitch!" yelled Sequoia getting in Zikhya's face. Zikhya threw a right and banged Sequoia in her mouth and watched as blood ran down her the side of her lip. Sequoia laughed like a crazed maniac. "Oh come on bitch, I know that's not ll you got!" she yelled as she two pieced Zikhya knocking her on the floor. "Bitch its nothing!" yelled Zikhya getting' up off the floor taking her fighting stance once again. "Bitch let's go then! You can quit now so your man don't see you get your ass whipped!" yelled Sequoia bouncing around like she was in a boxing ring. Zikhya tried to put her in a head lock and missed as Sequoia ducked, picked Zikhya up, and boduy slammed her on the kitchen floor. She put her gurads up and got back into boxing stance. "Damn, you on the floor again" she laughed as sweat poured down ̄ ̄ ̄ ̄ning down in between her breast "Sequoia, that's enough baby. You already whipped her ass, don't even waist your time on Raleigh. "Naw, fuck that, what's really good!" yelled Raleigh jumping up wildly. She got in her fighting stance leaving her whole face and chest area open just covering her face. Sequoia just stood there with her hands on her hips, looked at her, and laughed. "Raleigh, check this out. Just go home cause you don't eeven want this. Im not even going lie to you. " laughed Mo-T. Raleigh didn't listen and ended up being hit so hard by Sequoia that she slid underneath the kitchen cabinets that were underneath the sink. " That bitch snuck me!" yelled Raleigh. "Bitch, you got a nerve to fight on me when you was fucking the photographer in Las vegas. That wasn't no security room check! You think I'm fuckin stupid!" yelled Menijah as she held her swollen shut black eye. "WHAT! Bitch you goin go through all this and you fuckin niggas in Las Vegas!" yelled Mo-T. He walked back to the kitchen table and sat down with his head in his hands. Sequoia knew them bitches played dirty, so she knew it would come out. She stood there staring at Mo-T. "Um, I was going to tell you after…. " "YO, DON'T FUCKIN TALK TO ME BITCH! GET THE FUCK OUT MY FACE AND DON'T SAY SHIT TO ME RIGHT NOW!GET…THE…FUCK…OUT…MY…FACE!!!" he yelled as spit flew in Sequoia's face. She wiped her face, looked at Mo-T as tears slid down her eyes, and walked up the steps to get her things so she could leave. Mo-T paced back and forth in the kitchen as Raleigh, Zikhya, and Menijah struggled to get up off of the floor. "Mo-T can I use the phone to call Kendra?" asked Menijah. "BITCH FUCK YOU! DON'T SAY SHIT TO ME!" yelled Mo-T. Menijah became silent. "I'm sorry Mo-T, I have to go" said Sequoia as she came down the stairs with her clothes. "No, bitch. You staying here and you going tell me about this motha fuckin nigga you been fuckin!" yelled Mo-T as he grabbed Sequoai by the arm and pulled her back upstairs causing her to drop her luggage. Once they got inside their room, Mo-T slammed the door and began breaking and throwing every piece of furniture in the room. Sequoia was scared shitless. "How the fuck can you give my pussy away!" yelled Mo-T as he choked Sequoia up against the wall. "Mo-T I can't breath let me go. . " she said as she tried to pull his hands from around her neck. Mo-T looked her in her eyes as he continued to choke the life out of her. She started going in and out of consciousness, but Mo-T didn't care. "Bitch I should kill you and then kill myself. What the fuck do I have to live for now, huh!" he yelled as his grip tightened around her neck. He had a look on his face that she had never seen before and knew she was as good as dead. At this point, only one thing could save her. With the little bit of strength she had left, she managed to say the words that caused Mo-t to release his grip. "Mo-T, I'm pregnant" . Instantly his grip loosened and he let Sequoia fall to the floor. She rubbed her throat coughing and gasping for air. Mo-T was silent as he looked down at her. "How do I know it 's not that nigga seed?" he asked getting mad all over again. "I had missed my period before I went to Las Vegas, I was going to surprise you when I got back home. " said Sequoia. "Well bitch I still want a blood test. You aint my wife no fuckin more, you a slut just like the rest of them hoes downstairs" said Mo-T walking out of the room. Sequoia cried because she knew her husband had now lost all respect for her. Mo-T left out the door to clear his head. Meanwhile, Scar waited two blocks away watching the house waiting for Raleigh to make her exit. Sequoia gathered her thoughts and emotions before she made her way downstairs to leave. She saw Raleigh, Zikhya, and Menijah looking up at her as she made her way down the steps. The once tight friends sat staring at eachother and soon Menijah broke down crying. "What happened to us?" she sobbed. "Zikhya soon followed suit and suddenly they were all crying. " Ya'll tears are nothing compared to mine. Ya'll are some heartless bitches and I will never as long as I live forget this shit!" yelled Sequoia as she left out of the door without turning back.

Chapter Eleven

She headed back to Las Vegas with Torez and they had a ball. They got to know eachother a whole lot better and before she knew it, a year had flown by. As usual, he waited on her hand and foot, there were no females calling his home late night, and he introduced her to his whole family. Sequioa couldn't quite understand everything they were saying, but from the hospitality, she knew that they loved her to death. They hadsex every night, several times a night and Sequoia couldn't get enough of Torez. Meanwhile back in Baltimore, Zikhya was still chasing Mo-T while he chased other females. One day when he was leaving out of a girl named Elise house, he started his Escalade and noticed it sounded a little muffled when he turned it on. When he got out to check under the hood, he found sugar crumbs on his Engine Oil compartment. "I'M GOING KILL THAT CRAZY BITCH! He yelled as he kicked the side of his truck. He had the key to everything that belonged to Elise, so he jumped into her money green Lincoln Towncar and went straight to Zikhya's house. "BITCH, YOU WANNA PLAY CRAZY, I'LL SHOW YOU CRAZY!" yelled Mo-T as he went to the refrigerator and headed upstairs to Zikhya's bedroom. Zikhya was sleep, but not for long. Mo-T smeared jelly on her face, poured syrup on her hair, mustard and ketchup on her clothes, and dumped a whole jar of pickles on her head. "Aaaaarrrrgghhhhh! MOTHA FUCKA I'M GOING TO KILL YOU!" yelled Zikhya trying to catch her breath. Mo-T went outside to her car and did the same thing to hers that she did to his. Only he made her car look like her as well. He knew she was pregnant and he couldn't put his hands on her, so he did the next best thing; fucked up her hair and her car. Raleigh was still getting drunk and picking up guys from anywhere clueless to the fact that Tate had money on her head. Menijah in counseling because of depression and constantly having breakdowns. They all were leading different lives, but in the back of Menijah's mind she wanted everything to just go back to normal as if nothing happened. She prayed hard every single night, but it just seemed as if her prayers were going unanswered.

"Talk to me" . "Nigga what you sleep on duty? Yo you fuckin up, you can't let the bitch just slip away. I need somebody else on the job or what?" asked Tate angrily. "Naw, naw, naw son. It's not like that. I been watching the door like a hawk all night so I know shorty didn't come out at all. "You sure?" asked tate agitated. "Yeah man. I just went to sleep at four o'clock, it's only ten after four now. "Nigga in those ten minutes she could have slipped right past your ass! Look nigga, this is awhat you call a hit. This is not one of them bullshit beefs in the hood, this shit is real. This hit is personal and that's why it's so important for shit to go as I explained them to you. I asked you could you handle the job and you assured me that you could. I trusted your word so that means if my hit don't go through for any reason…. . " Tate paused, letting his words sink in, then hung up. Sacar knew what it was and he knew Tate was dead serious. Especially since he was from Mo-T's crew. It was all over the streets how Mo-T killed a police officer and got away with it, walking out of court a free man. To this day, Scar wondered how Mo-T pulled that off, but he wasn't trying to find out. "Hey, excuse me sweetheart!" Scar yelled at a pretty dark skinned girl sitting at a red light. The girl thought he was kind of cute and she liked what he was pushin' so she pulled over. "Wassup?" asked the girl as Scar leaned into her car window. "You a pretty girl and your gear is off the chain so I know you love money, right?" asked Scar. "Nigga get to the motha fuckin point" said the girl ready to pull off on Scar. "Ooooh, aggression, I like that" said Scar. The girl looked at him and rolled her eyes. "Alright, cuttin' the bullshit shorty I need a favor real wuick while I go to the gas station. See that house over there?" asked Scar pointing to Sequoia and zmo-T's house. "That's Mo-T's trifling ass house, what about it?" asked the girl. "You fucked Mo-t too? Damn!How come henever called me for none of this action?" joked Scar. "Who the fuck haven't had that all-around dick? That shit is old ews though, it's a new baller in town that got all us hoes on his dick, ya dig?" said the pretty girl. "Well ya'll not on my dick so fuck that and listen up cunt. I'm on a major stake out right now so I can't take my eyes off of that house for a second or that's my head" said Scar. "Okay, I follow you" said the girl seriously. "I'm going to the gas station and I need you to just sit here and guard that house to make sure nobody exit. If they do, I need you to odo this whistle code so I'll know wassup. I'm only going to that gas station across the way over there so I'll still be able to hear you, got it?" asked Scar. "Nigga that's not shit to do, I thought you had me fucked up like I was a trick or something" laughed the pretty girl. "You said it not me" laughed

Scar as he pulled off. The pretty girl put her middle finger up as she sipped on Grey Goose, listened to the radio, and watched the house. Half an hour later, she saw three females exit a house and knew at least one of them had to be his target. "Oh shit!" said the pretty girl noticing Raleigh. Elise's mom and Raleigh's mother used to get high together when they were just kids; way before Raleigh even knew Sequoia, Raleigh, and Menijah existed. She tried to put out a cigarette and burned her leg causing the horn to beep. Scar immediately looked over at the girl's car to see her squirming in her seat and brushing off her legs. He laughed as he made his way back across the street. "The job was too much for you to handle huh?" Scar smiled. "Man fuck that, I seen four bitches leave out of that house. Scar almost shitted on his self. "Why the fuck didn't you whistle the code bitch!" yelled Scar damn near slapping the pretty female for her stupidity. "As you can see, I almost set my own ass on fuckin fire and who the fuck you calling a bitch? You asked me for a mothafuckin favor! You know what, I'm out. " said the girl starting up her car. In reality, as soon as Scar pulled off she saw all four of the girls ball out, but she wasn't going to tell him that. She was a female so why would she rat another one out? They never did anything to her, not even Sequoia. "Bitch, turn that car off and get in here" said Scar pointing his glock at her head. The girl hit banged the dash board, and cursed her self. She promised not to help another motha fuckin ever again she saw just sitting on the side of the street. She now made a mental note that they were all up to no good. "My name is not bitch, it's Elise" she said climbing in the passenger seat of Scar's Lexus. "Bitch I don't give a fuck what your name is. You just did the dumb shit and I told you my life was on the line! So you going with me" said Scar pulling away from the curb with screeching tires. "Why you driving so fast and where you taking me?" Elise asked. "Sit back and enjoy the ride. We on a bounty hunt and if I go down, you going down with me" said Scar drinking his Red Bull energy drink. Elise was now scared shitless. When she stopped to help Scar, she didn't know that today could possibly be her last day living. She had family who loved her and would wonder where she was if she came up missing. Elise was only twenty year old, how could she have gotten herself in some big boy shit like this? She had to think of something and she had to think of something quick. "So what's your name?" she asked. "Mean-Green-Dick-Machine" said Scar. "Oh real cute" said Elise rolling her eyes. "Damn, this shit must be serious. He's not even giving me a clue about any information on him at all" she thought. She noticed a thick long Scar going from his temple to underneath his chin; somebody had cut the shit out of him. "What happened to your face?" she asked softly. "Oh that little shit? War wounds shoert, what you know about that? That shit don't face me, shit girl half of my face was hanging off and I still was busting my glocks. I didn't stop until all those bitches was laid down. Anybody in the motha fuckin way gets popped; grand mothers, kids whoever!" yelled Scar. It finally sunk in that Elise was in the company of a psychopath, she had to do something and she had to do it fast; but she was from the streets so snitching wasn't an option. While Scar was still distracted, she slowly put her hand on the passenger side door handle and flung the door open. She was grabbed back in the car by the back of her shirt as Scar swerved with the door wide open. "Shut the fuckin door now bitch or your brains will be all over this car!" yelled Scar.

In the middleof all the commotion, Tate called Scar and his auto answer system picked up on the call. Tate heard all the commotion in the background and knew it was Raleigh. "I got your ass now" he smiled as he hung up. He was interrupted by Coa-Coa calling him from downstairs. "Timothy, I know you hear me calling you! Guess who's here?" yelled Coa-Coa. "So girl how did the meeting go? That shit was like a year and a half ago and you haven't called me to tell me shit" said Coa-Coa hugging Sequoia. "Girl it was a mess, but I'ma Christian before I'm a woman. They cried, I cried. Hopefully today everybody can get closure and we can reunite as one so my heart is light with no burdens. I know one day I'll be blessed with a great husband and beautiful children one day soon. I'm not going to rush God's plans for me any longer, I'm going to be patient" said Sequoia. "Girl you mean to tell me you can live without dick! Shit I can't stay off of Tate. I want it more than he do. " Ya'll still carzy" . They both laughed as they sawTate entering the dining room. "What the fuck ya'll down here laughing at that's so funny? I know ya'll not trying to clown my nigga Mo-T?" asked Tate. "No, Tate, we are not clowning your boy. Actually I came back in town to discuss a serious mater with you concerning him" said Sequoia. "Some clowns tryna get at my nig, oh it's war time!" said Tate opening up a safe full of guns. "Timothy, you are so fucking embarrasng! Put that shit away, we have company!" yelled Coa-Coa trying to shut the safe. Sequoia stood there for a moment while they fought, but soon cleared her throat to make sure they didn't forget she was present. "Um, Coa-Coa, so you mind if I talk business to Tate in private?" asked Sequoia. "Oh girl hell no! You know you my girl, now if you were another bitch, I would have to cut you. That question is like disrespect where I'm from. You my Mami though so I trust you. Im going upstairs and call me if you need me to straighten his ass out" said Coa-Coa cutting her eyes at Tate. Sequoia laughed. "Girl fuck you, get your ass upstairs" said Tate. "Excatly, that's what I want you to do for me, but You keep running though" joked Coa-Coa as she ran upstairs. Sequoia was falling out in laughter. "Oh my goodness, ya'll are so cute. This is a duplicate of Mo-T and I "laughed Sequoia as she heard Coa-Coa shut the bedroom door behind her upastairs. Soon they heard her singing songs off of music videos. "That bitch is gone. On the real wassup with my boy though" asked Tate. "Nothing. Actually this is not about your boy" said Sequoia taking off her suit jacket. Tate looked at Sequoia with shocked raised eyebrows. "Nigga don't you even fucking think about it because you know I don't get down like that" said Sequoia as a matter of factly. "Girl, you had me excited for a minute" laughed Tate trying to hide the fact that his dick had instantly gotten hard. "Well calm your little wee-wee down because it's not that type of party" said Sequoia. "Yeah I see that. So what's really up?" asked Tate adjusting his boxers. "Call it off, Tate" said Sequoia. "What?'asked Tate. "Nigga you forgot I was with Mo-T's criminal minded ass for a long time. He taught me the streets and I know that shit like I know every g-string in my wardrobe. I saw Scar staking out in front of my house for hours that night, which is why I chose to leave my house and let them stay that night. I heard about what happened, so call it off. "It's too late" smiled Tate. Sequoia opened her cellphone as Tate watched her and dialed a number. She then put the phone in speaker mode. "Hey girl, what you doing?" Sequoia asked the person on the other end. "Girl, I'm chillin' with these niggas I just met at the car wash. They cool as a motha fucka" laughed Raleigh. Tate couldn't believe his ears. "Alright, I'll talk to you later" said Sequoia. " Oh ya'll cool now?" asked Tate. "Tate you keep your friends close, and your enemies closer. Im a smart female. Raleigh know what she did was wrong so she felt guilty. I used her to my advantage and the entire time I was in Las Vegas she was giving me the scoop about what was happening down here in Baltimore and I didn't even have to ask;she was leaving it on my voicemail. I had to call her back when she told me about Zikhya putting sugar under Mo-T's hood" laughed Sequoia. "Who was the bitch I heard him cursing out in the back ground when I called then when he was telling her to shut the car door before he killed her?" asked Tate. "Boy that was one of Mo-T's hoes, Elise" said Sequoia. "What the fuck was she doing in the car with Scar" Tate asked now angry realizing that a sheet had been pulled over

Scar's eyes by a bitch. "From what I saw, it looked like he had her staking out while he went to get something to wake himself up. Apparently home girl fucked up because we all slipped away without her knowing until the last minute" said Sequoia She didn't mention the fact that Raleigh knew Elise because she knew that Tate would try to find a way to kill her through Sequoia. "I want to kill that motha fucka!" yelled Tate balling his fist up. "Tate, please do this for me. If you let Raleigh live, I promise you won't have any more problems out of her. I'm sending her back home to Georgia so she can get her life back together, please Tate?" begged Sequoia as she stood up and grabbed Tate's hand looking him dead in his face. Suddenly Tate kissed her and she jumped back out of shock. The two of them stood silent as they stared at each other; that's when they heard it. "Aaaarrrgggghhh! My water broke!

Coa-Coa had a healthy nine pound and eight ounces baby boy. She named him Timothy Gray, III. Tate was a proud man and it showed. He couldn't stop smiling. Sequoia, Tate, Mo-T, Raleigh, Menijah, and Zikhya were all surrounding Coa-Coa and the baby in the GBMC hospital. Even though it had been a year since they had all saw each other, everyone looked the same as she remembered; besides Zikhya putting on a little weight in her waist and thigh area. It looked as if her breast had grown huger than they already were too. Sequoia was glad everyone could come together as family once again. It was like the baby had changed everybody's purpose in life. Sometimes, children had a way of doing just that. Sequoia knew that in order for the baby to have a normal life, all of the drama had to cease. What happened between Sequoia and Tate would stay between them, but Sequoia was happy that Tate changed his mind about killing Raleigh. Sequoia knew it was because of his new born son that he had been waiting on for a long time. Sequoia was not out of the back stabbing breed, so she knew she wasn't going to do Coa-Coa crudy. She wanted to tell her, but it would only start up more drama and confusion all over a kiss and nothing more. Sequoia didn't feel anything for Tate, it was just a mistake. Besides, she wasn't about to have two best friends beefing knowing how ruthless they both were. A lot of females thought it was cute to have two guys going to war over them, but that shit wasn't cute at all. Sequoia wouldn't be able to live with herself if she had either one of their blood on her hands. She forgave everybody who had done her wrong and moved on. Although her and Mo-T had a baby girl on the way, they still weren't getting back together. They did promise eachother to be the best of friends though. "Awww, look at all that pretty hair!"

cued Zikhya. "I know and he look like a little chink!" cued Raleigh. "I can't get over all that hair either!" said Menijah. "Man, back up off that man nut sack. He the new gangsta of Baltimore City streets" said Mo-T picking up Lil Tate. "Mo-T stop cursing all loud before they put us out" said Sequoia hitting him on his back. "Girl you know what you hittin?That's iron steel back there girl" said Mo-T passing thebaby to Tate and flexing his muscles. Everybody started laughing. Sequoia rolled her eyes and had to laugh at Mo-T herself. He was a pure natural jack ass and that was one thing she used to love most about her husband. He was always the center of attention. "Yeah she know it's steel Mo-T cause in a few months she going be laid up just like Coa-Coa" laughed Tate. "Oh Tate so you got jokes now? See the next plate I fix you because you know Coa-Coa can't cook until she heal from having the baby nigga" said Sequoia. "Oh come on girl, don't do this to ya boy! It's ya boy baby! This me, Tay-ski!" yelled Tate as everybody laughed. "Alright ladies, ya'll hold Tate Junior while the fellas go roll up. We be back" said Mo-T as Tate kissed Coa-Coa and the baby leaving the girls alone. "So how do you feel being pregnant for the first time?" Coa-Coa asked Sequoia. "I mean, it feels strange. I'm excited, but I'm scared I'm going to loose this sexy ass body" said Sequoia looking at herself in the mirror. "Girl, pregnant bodies are the sexiest bodies out there. Watch how many niggas be trying to holla at you" said Coa-Coa. Zikhya, Raleigh, and Menijah laughed. "They better do it when Mo-t not around because for some reason he think we still together" said Sequoia. "I'm glad he didn't take it as far as going forward with the blood test. That shit is humiliating" said Zikhya trying to throw salt in the game. "Girl, he better not. Shit, I'm wifey" said Sequoia switching across the room. They all laughed at her.

"Man, my head is fucked up right now" said Mo-T smoking the blunt. "What's up nigga, talk to me" said Tate. " You know that bitch Zikhya called me lastnight talking about she's pregnant. "Tate's eyes almost popped out of his head. "Yeah nigga, her and Sequoia only a few weeks apart yo. They both told me time frames and right now, it's not looking good for ya boy" said Mo-T passing the blunt to Tate. "Nigga tell that bitch to get rid ofthat baby yo, fuck that" said Tate coughing. "Naw man, I want a boy like you; to carry on my name" said Mo-T. "Okay nigga then after Sequoia have the girl, try again. You aint saying nothing" said Tate. Mo-T laughed. "Awwwww man, you got feelings for the bitch?" asked tate. "It's like this man. When ya'll look at Zikhya, ya'll see a freak, somebody who fucked everybody in the neighborhood, which she did. I got to know her man and it's so much more to her . I know that I'm the only nigga who even acted like I cared about her. I didn't just fuck her and send her on her way. Remember when you fucked them up?" Mo-T asked Tate. "Yeah, you talkin about when I slapped thefire out of them bitches" asked Tate. Mo-T laughed, " Yeah. She told me that she knew that was my way of showing her attention" said Mo-T. "Ooohhh shit! You got a crazy bitch!" laughed Tate. "Exactly nigga and if I tell her to get rid of the baby she might try to start some bullshit all over again. I don't want that since everything is kind of back to normal, you feel me?" asked Mo-T. "So you going be with Zikhya too?" asked Tate. "Hell no nigga, I'm pretending" said Mo-T. Tate started laughing his ass off. "Yo Sequoia looking kind of good my nig. If you don't grab her, I might have to steal that shorty" joked Tate. "Nigga I will blow your fucking brains out over my bitch. You my boy, but when it come to that bitch, I'll put you to rest my nig. You gangsta, but you know you not fuckin with me nigga. Not ot mention I layed that nest in that pa-dussy. Shit nigga I put you down" said Mo-T passing Tate the roach. Everything Mo-T was saying, Tate knew was true;which was why he nodded his head with respect. Just then Zikhya came outside. "Me and Sequoia are hungry. We want some Mo's Seafood" said Zikhya holding her stomach. She agitated Mo-T when she did that. She was always so extra with her shit. "Ya'll hoes got feet, start walking" said Mo-T. The weed had fully taken affect on Tate and he was rollin at everything Mo-T said. "Morton Wallace, don't play with me" said Zikhya folding her arms. "What ya'll hoes want, this dick with a side of balls?" he joked. Tate was laughing so hard he couldn't breath. "Yo, Mo-T stop yo! Stop man, my stomach hurt!" yelled Tate. "Stop playiiing" whined Zikhya. "Sike what ya'll want, forreal" said Mo-T pretending to be serious. "I want…" Zikhya didn't get a chance to finish because Mo-T pulled off in the parking garage. He turned the car around and stopped in front of a now mad Zikhya. After he stopped laughing he asked her what her and Sequoia wanted from the store. "Alright, bet. I be back" said Mo-T "Give me a kiss" said Zikhya leaning in the window to get a kiss. As soon as she was close to Mo-T's lips, he pulled off and left this time.

"I'll be back ya'll. I have to make a phone call" said Sequoia leaving the room. Zikhya passed her as she was leaving. "You gone? I just sent Mo-T to get the food" said Zikhya. "oh no, I'm using my cell phone. I'm coming back in the room in am minute" said Sequoia. "oh okay" said Zikhya quickly calling Mo-T to make sure he wasn't on the phone with Sequoia. " Talk to me?" Mo-T answered. "Who you on the phone with?"

asked Zikhya. " I'm not on the fuckin phone Zikhya, don't be calling me with that dumb shit. You enough problems by your damn self" said Mo-T hanging up on her. Meanwhile, Sequoia called Torez because she hadn't spoken to him since she left out of Las Vegas that morning. "I've been waiting on your call" said Torez. "I know. So what are you doing?" asked Sequoia. "Worried about you" said Torez. There was silence. "Um, hey listen, I'm going to book a flight tonight to the yacht. I need to talk to you about some things, but I need to do it face to face" said Sequoia. "Fine gorgeous. Call me when you touch down. I can't wait to see you. Oh yeah and…" "I know Torez, wear something sexy. You should already know you do not have to tell me that" sassed Sequoia. "I know, I'm just fucking with you" They both laughed and Sequoia hung up and returned to Coa-Coa's room. Everybody was stuffing their faces, except for Coa-Coa . Mo-T and Taqte must have entered Coa-Coa's room through the other side because she sure didn't see them walk past her. "Niggas and short cuts" she thought. Even Lil Tate was sucking on a french fry that Tate put in his mouth. "Timothy you can't do that he's just a baby, plus you smell just like weed so move!" yelled Coa-Coa. "This is my fucking son and I can do what I want. If it wasn't for me cunt, you wouldn't have him" said Tate making everybody laugh. "She just mad because she can't have this food" laughed Zikhya. For some reason Zikhya was sitting extra close to Mo-t, but he wasn't Sequoia's man any longer so she dimissed the thought. Everybody was eating something different, it was crazy. Zikhya had steamed shrimp and Sequoia had to admit that she was knocking them shrimp down! Menijah had a Big Mac meal from McDonalds with a strawberry milkshake, Raleigh had Chinese food, Tate was smashing a chicken and steak enchilada from Taco Bell, Mo-T had goat smothered in rice with gravy from the Jamaican spot over West Baltimore. "Dig in baby" said Mo-T when he saw Sequoia come in the room. Zikhya gave him a funny look, but kept quiet. "Uh, you know what? I think I'll take mine to go" said Sequoia picking up the bag with the Seafood fettuchini inside. "Why Sequoia, eat with us. This is the moment we've all been waiting to get back. We're like family again, please?" asked Coa-Coa. She was still emotionally unstabled because her hormones weren't back to normal yet. "Well, I um…" She didn't want to say she had to be somewhere because she knew Mo-T would lay her ass out. Even though they came to an understanding that they weren't together as a couple, in a sense they still were. She didn't know why she was still scared to say or do anything around Mo-T. She just wasn't the type of female to say "Fuck him, it's over. I'm doing me" in a matter of days. Her love for her husband was and always will be real. She couldn't fool her self; she was still in love with Mo-T. Now that she was pregnant by him, she loved him even more. The problem was that she was starting to love Torez too. Knowing the type of person she was, she knew she had to truth and that's what she was going to do; after she fucked Torez fine ass one more good time! "Let me holla at you for a minute Sequoia" said Mo-T jumping up to follow Sequoia out the door. Zikhya shot daggers at Sequoia and Sequoia shrugged her shoulders and looked at her as if to say:" What do you want me to do? I can't control him" . Once they got inside Sequoia's car, Mo-T let her have it. "Bitch, you still my wife, you still my girl. Go ahead and fuck that nigga one last time, tell him his over, and bring that ass back home. I love you, give me a kiss, be safe and goodbye" said Mo-T getting out of the car. Sequoia opened her mouth, but nothing came out, so she just closed it. That was the part of Mo-T that turned her on. Her husband had swagger in the worst way. Her panties instantly got wet as she watched him. " Damn he even bop sexy" she thought as she waited for him to disappear into the hospital before pulling off.

"I brought you something" said Torez as he took Sequoia's coat and hung it up as soon as she stepped through the door. "What is it?" asked Sequoia sipping the glass of wine he poured for her also. "I'll tell you later, but first let's talk" said Torez. "Okay" said Sequoia swallowing a lump in her throat. "Why are you so damn sexy?" asked Torez. Sequoia fell out laughing. This was the part she loved about Torez. He was always making her smile. "Okay, okay. Stop playing and tell me what you really want to talk about" said Sequoia. Torez suddenly grabbed a small box out of his back pocket and dropped to his knees. Sequoia put her hand over her chest as if she was having a heart attack. When Torez opened the box, she almost fainted at the size of the wedding ring. "Sequoia, I have loved you since the first day I met you. When you are not here with me, I feel you in my spirit. I prayed to GOD for you to come back to me when you were away in Baltimore today. I' am empty without you. Those words are words of a man who is in love. Will you, Sequoia Birmingham take me, Torez Utopia to be your husband, please?" he added giving her a puppy face. Sequoia couldn't lie, the wedding ring that Mo-T bought her looked like shit compared to the one that was in front of her face. It was so big, Sequoia don't think she could have fit her hand in her purse ever again. She wasn't going to let a ring break her bond with her husband, besides; a lot of consequences might come with accepting that ring. Even under pressure, she had to think smart. To avoid answering him, she tongue kissed him. Torez slid the ring on Sequoia's finger while they were kissing. "Damn, this ring is fit for a queen! I can knock a bitch out with this" she said as Torez began to undress her. Another thing she loved about Torez was that he wasn't too rough, but he wasn't too soft either. It was like he had just the right amount of roughness when the time came, but he knew when to be gentle as well. From the first time, Sequoia never had to show him what she liked, he knew automatically. That made her think they were definitely meant to be, but the way she felt for her husband even after what he did let her know that what she felt for Torez was only from Mo-T hurting her. Who is to say Mo-T won't do anything else? Sequoia didn't know the answer to that, but she did know that she still loved her husband and that she was going to follow her heart. That night, she fucked Torez like her life depended on it. It was like she turned into a sex crazed animal and Torez loved it. Sequoia's hair was flying every where, she was sweating, and sucking Torez fingers. One thing she never did the entire time they were messing around was put her mouth on his penis. She had to give herself that, she didn't go around sucking anybody's dick. That was her first time cheating and even if it wasn't, she just didn't get down like that. When she thought about it, it always seemed like when Torez got in her pussy, he forgot all about getting his dick sucked. He had asked once, but after he got in her wet-wet, he forgot all about it. "Oh girl, your pussy is too good for you to have" moaned Torez as he felt Sequoia's cum running down his leg. "How you stay so wet?" he asked her. "Don't worry about all that, just give me that hard dick baby. Fuck this pussy tonigt and fuck it hard!" yelled Sequoia backing her big ass up on him. "Girl stop, you going make me cum" It was no use; Sequoia was in her own world as she pulled on Torez hair and kept cuming on his dick. The whole bed was wet. "Oh my Goodness Sequoia! What the fu…. AAAAAHHHHHHHH!" yelled Torez as he came inside of her. Sequoia bit her lip and smiled as she pushed Torez dick out of her and stepped in the shower. "Awwww man. Girl, girl girl girl!" he sang as he got a towel to wipe the sweat off of his face and body. By the time Sequoia got out of the shower, Torez was snoring like a new born baby. She quietly slid the ring off and sat it on the night stand. She wrote him a brief note before she left:

My Dearest Torez,

The time that I spent with you since we met have been the best days of my life in all the years I have been married to my husband. You have lots of qualities about you that made me want to say yes and give you my hand in marriage. However, let's be real; if I was married to you and pregnant with your child, would you want me to marry another man who was just a fuck? I think we both know the answer to that. I mean, you caught me when I was lonely, confused, and hurt. I wasn't emotionally stabled at those moments. At first, I had no answers or explanations, but now I do. I'm not happy about what happened, but my heart feels lighter now that I have heard all sides to the story. I want to make it work with my husband because that's where my heart is, but your sex was outstanding!

Take care of your self and I really thank you for being there for me in my time of need. May God bless you!

Spiritually Yours Forever,

Mrs. "Why are you so sexy" Wallace...LOL

Torez cried like baby when he read that note and realized that the ring was still on the table. He felt like he had been stabbed in his heartand had no sense of what he would do next. He set his whole future in the palm of Sequoia's hands because he just knew she would accept his proposal. Now that she didn't, he didn't know what direction to turn in.

Chapter Twelve

"So Raleigh, you ready for the big move?" asked Sequoia as she watched her pack her belongings. "Yeah, I guess. I'm just going to miss ya'll. You know we've always been four strong" said Raleigh sadly. "We know that Raleigh, but too much crazy shit has happened down here in Baltimore. If I were you, I would consider this a second chance of life instead of looking sad" said Zikhya. That was the best thing Zikhya had ever said since Sequoia had known her. "I hate to say it, but she is absolutely right. I mean, you almost weren't here" said Sequoia. "If I had family that was outside of Baltimore and they told me I'm welcomed anytime, girl you think I wouldn't hop on that?" asked Menijah. Zikhya who are you texting all that time over there?" asked Raleigh. "I know she over there making love to the phone and shit" said Menijah trying to snatch the phone from her. "Damn, is Sequoia the only one who know's how to mind her business around here?" joked Zikhya. "I sure do girl, because I have a baby to worry about. She yawned. This baby been kicking my butt, she is going to be a handful just like her daddy. " said Sequoia as she rubbed her belly. The baby kicked and it startled her. "What, is something wrong?" asked Menijah as she noticed the way Sequoia jumped. Sequoia laughed. "No girl, she kicked and I didn't expect it to be that hard. See feel it" said Sequoia lifting up her blouse and putting Menijah's hand on her stomach. It took everything in Zikhya not to say anything about her own pregnancy so she left out the house and slammed the door. "What's wrong with her?" asked Raleigh. "You don't worry about that, you pack. I'll be sitting in the car" said Sequoia. As she was walking to her car, she heard Zikhya outside on the phone yelling at someone. "It's not fucking fair! I'm tired of everything that has to do with me being a secret!" she yelled. "Mmmmmm, must be somebody else's husband" mumbled Sequoia as she sat in her car and listened to Keyshia Cole waiting for Raleigh.

To say that the ride to Georgia from Baltimore was a long trip would be an understatement. It was well worth it though, Sequoia loved the homey feeling she received from the people of Georgia. It was so much different than hatin' ass Baltimore. You would never see a bunch of females hanging in groups of fifteen in Baltimore without there being a fight. Bitches down there hated on eachother too much. When Sequoia pulled up in front of Raleigh's destination, she had a whole porch filled with family waiting for her" "Ohhhh lawd, how you durn chile. Antie Mabel aint seened you since you was high as my knee. Give me some shugas baby" Sequoia laughed as Raleigh eyes got big while a big boned Mrs. Mabel squeezed her tight. "Oh this musta be ha freend cuz you sho caint be famila wit' all that jonk een yo truck" said Uncle Herb. "Oh Herb quit cutna fool" said Aunt Mabel. "Go on and put yo thangs inside honey. Antie Mabel cooking some pigs feet, hamhocks, turkey necks, chicken and dumplings, catfish, fried chicken, corn on the cob, fresh collard greens, sweet potatoes, peas, chili and cornbread, mashed potatoes drowned in gravy, left over po chops and a side of apple pie" said Antie Mabel. "Damn can I stay" laughed Sequoia, but she was dead serious. "Oh you stayin sugar britches, let me gone and show ya yo room; it's right next ta mine" said Uncle Herb as he smiled so wide that Sequoia saw every single gap and rotten tooth he had in his mouth. "Come to think about it, I have to get home before my husband kill sme. Tell Raleigh to call me Antie Mabel" said Sequoia damn near running to her car. "Oh yo husband to come to" yelled Uncle Herb, but Sequoia was already pulling off headed back to Baltimore. As sson as she got on the beltway, she got acall from Mo-T. She figured he didn't want anything so she pressed the ignore button. Strangely, he kept calling back so she answered the fifth time. "Hello?" "Sequoia, baby I'm at GBMC" said Mo-T out of breath. Sequoia almost fainted and lost control of the steering wheel. She quickly pulled over and sipped on the cold Deer Park bottled water she grabbed out of Aunt Mabels cooler. Sequoia, baby you there?" asked Mo-T. "Are you alright? Please say you're alright!" cried Sequoia starting to hyperventilate. I'm good; it's not me" said Mo-T sadly. "Hold the fuck up! I know it better not be Raleigh because I told Tate's ass to let that shit go. He promised me he would right before Coa-Coa's watr broke!" yelled Sequoia getting upset. She knew just as fast as she dropped Raleigh off;she could have a hit put on her in Georgia an dbe dead within seconds. Tha was how Mo-T and his crew rolled; they eyes and ears everywhere. "Sequoia it's Zikhya. She lost my baby……" .

TO BE CONTINUED... Bitch we can Share PART II IS COMING SOON!